Closed for the Season

OTHER GRIPPING STORIES BY
MARY DOWNING HAHN

All the Lovely Bad Ones

Deep and Dark and Dangerous

The Old Willis Place

Time for Andrew

The Doll in the Garden

Wait Till Helen Comes

MARY DOWNING HAHN

Closed FOR the Season

A Mystery Story

Clarion Books
Houghton Mifflin Harcourt
Boston • New York
2009

Clarion Books
215 Park Avenue South
New York, NY 10003
Copyright © 2009 by Mary Downing Hahn

The text was set in 11-point Charter.

Clarion Books is an imprint of Houghton Mifflin Harcourt Publishing Company.

www.clarionbooks.com

Printed in the United States of America

Library of Congress Cataloging-in-Publication Data

Hahn, Mary Downing.
Closed for the season : a mystery / by Mary Downing Hahn.
p. cm.
Summary: When thirteen-year-old Logan and his family move into a
run-down old house in rural Virginia, he discovers that a woman was
murdered there and becomes involved with his neighbor Arthur in a
dangerous investigation to try to uncover the killer.
ISBN 978-0-547-08451-0
[1. Mystery and detective stories. 2. Murder—Fiction. 3. Neighbors—Fiction.
4. Friendship—Fiction. 5. Virginia—Fiction.] I. Title.
PZ7.H1256Cl 2009
[Fic]—dc22
2008046846

QUM 10 9 8 7 6 5 4 3 2 1

FOR JAMES CROSS GIBLIN

Editor, mentor, and friend
for thirty years

Closed for the Season

By the time Dad pulled into the driveway of our new house, all I wanted was to go inside and jump in the shower. If we had a shower, that is. Or even any water. Dad had warned us the house needed a lot of work, but the place was in worse shape than I'd imagined, old and run-down, paint peeling and flaking, a broken downspout dangling from the eaves, old papers littering the porch. The grass was at least two feet high, choked with towering thistles and milkweed. The bushes and trees had a wild, shaggy look. Mom, who'd described it as a quaint Victorian cottage "with tons of potential," grew strangely quiet at the sight of it.

Dad took one look, sighed, and opened the car door. "It seems the realtor forgot to have someone mow the lawn." He shook his head and sighed again. "It's a good thing I don't start teaching until fall. We have some time to get this place in shape."

"Please don't tell me this is our house," I said to Mom. "We aren't *really* going to live here. It's Dad's idea of a joke—right?"

Making a big effort to infuse her voice with enthusiasm, Mom said, "For heaven's sake, Logan, wait till it's painted and the lawn's cut. It will be adorable."

With a cynical sigh, I followed my parents toward the front door. A black mutt about the size of a German shepherd watched us from the porch. Mom edged behind Dad, but there was no need to be scared. The dog got to his feet and wagged his tail as if he was greeting old friends.

"Does he come with the house?" I asked.

Mom eyed the dog as if she suspected his friendliness was an act. "I think he belongs to the people next door."

As if on cue, a boy appeared at the hedge separating his yard from ours. "His name's Bear," he said. "Part rottweiler, part lab. He used to belong to the lady who lived in your house, but now he's mine and Grandma's."

The boy and I stared at each other over the low hedge. He was shorter than I was—younger, too. Probably no more than eleven. His straight yellow hair hung in his eyes and straggled down the back of his neck, his glasses were held together with tape, and he wore a faded T-shirt big enough for Dad that said, MENZER'S HARDWARE—IF WE DON'T HAVE IT, YOU DON'T NEED IT.

"I've been waiting all day for you." The boy frowned as if he expected me to apologize for inconveniencing him. "Grandma was sure you'd be here by noon, and it's almost six o'clock." He held up a skinny arm to show me the time on an enormous watch that was way too big for his bony wrist.

I'd been trapped in the back seat of an un-air-conditioned car for almost two hours. The temperature was over ninety. I was hot, I was tired, I was in a really bad mood. I definitely did not feel like being friendly. Especially with such a weird-looking kid.

"My name's Arthur Jenkins," the boy went on. "What's yours?"

"Logan Forbes." I glanced over my shoulder, hoping to see Mom or Dad beckoning me to come inside and help unpack or something. But no one was in sight. Now, if I'd *wanted* to stay outside and talk to Arthur Jenkins, you can bet my parents would have been hollering at me to get my butt in the house.

"How old are you?" Arthur asked. Without giving me a chance to answer, he said, "I'm almost twelve. Next fall I'll be in sixth grade at Oak View Middle School. You can't really see any oaks from there because they cut them all down to build a bunch of big expensive houses. Fair Oaks, it's called, in memory of the trees, I guess. Mostly everyone our age lives there. They're all snobs."

"I turned thirteen last month," I said. "I'll be in seventh grade, a whole year ahead of you."

Arthur shrugged. "We can be friends anyway. Living so close—that's propinquity." He paused to see if I knew what "propinquity" meant. In case I didn't, he added, "That means proximity or nearness. Also kinship and similarity in nature." He flashed a crooked grin. "I have the biggest vocabulary in my grade. I'm also the best speller and the best reader. I read five hundred and three books for last year's read-a-thon. Not Dr. Seuss, either—thick ones, like the Harry Potter books. I won so much free pizza, I don't even like the way it smells anymore."

While Arthur bragged, I looked longingly at the house. I could hear Dad hammering, but no one came to the door to call me inside.

Arthur pulled a stick of gum out of his pocket. Without offering me any, he stuffed it in his mouth. I watched him chew with lip-smacking relish, blow a big bubble, and suck it slowly back inside his mouth.

When he was ready to talk again, he said, "You've got some nice furniture. Expensive, Grandma says. We watched the moving men carry it in yesterday. How big is your TV screen? I've never seen one that size except in a store down at Peckham Mall."

I shrugged and glanced at the house, still hoping someone would rescue me from Arthur.

"Grandma and I didn't think anybody was ever going to buy old Mrs. Donaldson's place," Arthur went on. "It's been empty for almost three years. I guess the real estate company was hoping some folks from out of town like you-all would buy it without knowing what happened in it."

He paused to blow another bubble.

"What do you mean?" I asked, curious in spite of myself. "What happened in our house?"

He leaned across the hedge, his face so close I could smell his gum. "Mrs. Donaldson died there. . . . She was *murdered*."

"Murdered?" I stared at Arthur, shocked. "No way."

"Ask Grandma. She's the one who found her." His eyes widened behind the smeared lenses of his glasses. In a low voice, he went on with what I hoped was a story he'd concocted to scare me.

"One night, Bear woke up Grandma and me, barking like he'd gone crazy or something. We both kept hoping he'd shut up so we could go back to sleep, but he didn't stop. Finally, Grandma went downstairs, and I followed her. Bear was at our back door, making a horrible fuss." Arthur paused and glanced at the dog, who'd raised his head at the mention of his name.

"Mrs. Donaldson never let him out unless he was on a leash," Arthur went on. "Not only that, his head was bleeding, like somebody had whacked him hard enough to kill an ordinary dog." He paused again, and I found myself staring at Bear, who was now scratching his ear.

Arthur sighed. "Grandma and I knew something was wrong. It was one of those weird feelings—you know what I mean?"

I nodded. "Like in a movie, when the music gets scary and you can tell something bad is going to happen?"

"Exactly." Arthur crossed his arms across his skinny chest and took a deep breath. "Grandma told me to stay inside while she ran to Mrs. Donaldson's house. The back door was wide open, and the kitchen was a wreck. Drawers emptied out, stuff strewn everywhere, furniture turned over. Bear ran down the cellar steps, whining and crying, and Grandma followed him. Mrs. Donaldson was lying on the floor. Dead."

Despite the warm summer sun, goose bumps raced up and down my arms. "Maybe she just fell down the steps, maybe—"

"Even the police said it was murder," Arthur interrupted. "Somebody broke in and killed her. Then they tore the whole house apart—not just the kitchen, but every room, including the attic. They were looking for money, I guess."

I glanced at Bear, who'd gone back to sleep on our porch. "Is he really her dog?"

"Mrs. Donaldson loved that dog, and he loved her. He must have done his best to protect her. But . . ." Arthur shrugged. "The cops were going to take him to the pound, but Grandma said we'd keep him. The sad thing is he spends more time at your house than ours. I guess he's hoping Mrs. Donaldson will come back someday."

While Arthur talked, I found myself staring at my new home. Before I'd learned its gruesome secret, it had seemed like an ordinary little house, kind of homely and run-down. Now it had a sinister look, as if it were hiding behind the overgrown trees and bushes, keeping dark, scary secrets.

Our back door opened then, and Mom leaned out. "Logan, how about giving us some help in here?"

At the same moment, a woman appeared on Arthur's porch. Like him, she was skinny as a stick. Her hair was blond or white, I wasn't sure which, and it stuck up like a cockatoo's crest. Her eyebrows were black, drawn on a little too high, which gave her face a startled look. I didn't have any idea how old she was—anywhere from middle-aged to ancient was the closest I could guess.

"Hello, there," she called to me. "Welcome to Bealesville. I'm Arthur's granny, Darla Jenkins. Tell your folks I'll come on over for a visit after they get settled."

To Arthur she said, "Dinner's ready, Artie. Come in and wash up."

"See you later." Without another word, Arthur ran to his house, which was smaller and in worse need of paint than ours. Taking the sagging steps two at a time, he yanked open the screen door and disappeared.

In the sudden silence, I heard his grandmother say, "Arthur Jenkins, how often must I tell you not to slam that door!"

I headed for our house, eager to confront Mom and Dad with the truth about our new home.

As soon as I entered the kitchen, I blurted out, "Why didn't you tell me the old woman who used to live in this house was murdered here?"

Mom looked up from the pots and pans she was trying to organize. "What are you talking about?"

"Who told you that?" Dad asked at the same time.

"The boy next door. Arthur. His grandmother found the body. Down there." I pointed to the cellar door. "At the bottom of the steps."

"Mrs. Donaldson did die of a fall down those steps," Dad said slowly. "But she wasn't murdered, Logan."

"We thought it might worry you to know someone died here," Mom put in. "We should have known you'd hear it from somebody else—with embellishments."

"Worry me?" I repeated. "It's bad enough she died, but she was *murdered,* Mom. K-I-L-L-E-D. That definitely worries me!"

"She wasn't—" Mom began, but the doorbell interrupted her.

"That must be the pizza I ordered," Dad said.

We followed him to the front door, and, sure enough, a

guy holding a pizza box stood on the porch. While Dad went through the business end of the delivery, the pizza guy said, "I'm glad to see somebody's finally moved into poor old Mrs. Donaldson's house. It's been empty for a long time. I guess it was hard to sell, considering what happened—"

"Yes, the place has really been neglected," Dad broke in before the delivery guy could finish. "I've got my work cut out for me."

"If you need any help, just let me know," the pizza guy said. "My name's Johnny O'Neil." He scribbled something on a card from the pizza place and handed it to Dad. "Here's my phone number. I work nights at Golden Joe's Pizza Go-Go, so I'm free in the daytime."

"How are you with a lawn mower?" Dad gestured at the weedy yard.

"No problem," Johnny answered. "I can cut the grass to-morrow, if you like. Twenty dollars front and back, guaranteed neat job. I used to do it for Mrs. Donaldson before—"

"Great." Dad grinned. "How about ten A.M.?"

"It's a deal."

We watched Johnny run to his car, which sported a big pizza sign on the roof, and drive away fast. No doubt some hungry family was wondering where their pizza was.

"Why do you think Johnny said 'poor old Mrs. Donaldson?'" I asked Mom.

She handed me a slice of pizza loaded with all the things I love—mushrooms, sausage, pepperoni, and extra cheese—and shrugged. "Probably because she died, Logan."

Turning to Dad, she said. "Did you notice his tattoos?"

"Really professional work," Dad said, totally missing the tone of disapproval in Mom's voice. "The detail and color, the intricacy—"

"He'll be sorry when he's older," Mom interrupted. Giving me a sharp look, she added, "I hear it's a very painful and expensive process to have tattoos removed."

I'd been thinking Johnny's tattoos were pretty cool, but I decided to keep that thought to myself.

"I hope he shows up tomorrow," Mom went on to Dad. "He doesn't look like the responsible type."

His mouth full of pizza, Dad simply shrugged.

Just as I helped myself to the last slice, I heard a footstep in the kitchen. I whirled around, half expecting to see Mrs. Donaldson's ghost, but it was only Arthur standing in the dining room doorway, holding a cake.

"My grandmother sent this to welcome you," he told Mom. "It's devil's food with chocolate icing, the best you ever ate. She'd have brought it herself, but her hip's bothering her."

Since Arthur was practically drooling, Mom invited him to join us for dessert. In one second, he was sitting beside me, holding a fork, watching Mom cut into the cake. "Don't tell Grandma," he said. "I'm not supposed to have any. She told me it's all for you."

"Your secret's safe with us." Mom handed Arthur the first piece, intending him to pass it down to Dad, but he kept it for himself. Before Mom had the second slice cut, Arthur had his mouth full.

I guessed the word "etiquette" and its definition were missing from his enormous vocabulary.

As we ate, we learned more about our house than we wanted to know. According to Arthur's grandma, the back yard flooded every time it rained, the roof was in bad shape (and no doubt leaked), and the porch suffered from dry rot.

"Termites, too, most likely," Arthur said gloomily. "Mrs. Donaldson was getting too old to keep up with the repairs. Grandma says the place is about to fall down."

Dad smiled a little stiffly. "We had the house looked at before we moved in, Arthur. The inspector gave it a clean bill of health."

"Was it Mr. Lacey?"

When Dad nodded, Arthur looked glum. "Grandma says Errol G. Lacey would rather stand outside in the rain and lie than come in the house and tell the truth. He is positively and absolutely mendacious. She wouldn't trust him as far as she can throw him—which isn't very far, because he must weigh at least three hundred pounds stark naked."

Mom flashed a worried look at Dad, but he was studying our neighbor as if he were an unknown species. Unaware of Dad's scrutiny, Arthur accepted another piece of cake and lit into it with relish.

"I saw Johnny O'Neil deliver a pizza to your house," he said through a mouthful of crumbs. "I bet it was cold. He always stops and talks to people. Grandma doesn't know how Joe stays in business with Johnny doing the deliveries. Must be lots of folks like cold pizza."

He paused to lick the icing off his fingers. "I guess it's be-cause Johnny is Joe's nephew. Plus Golden Joe's is the only pizza place in town. Not that I'd ever eat there. The health department's after Joe big-time. Roaches in the kitchen, rats—"

Seeing that Mom was turning greenish, Dad cut into Arthur's monologue. "What's this story you told Logan about Mrs. Donaldson being murdered?"

"It's true," Arthur replied. "Ask anybody. Someone broke in and pushed her down the steps. They almost killed her dog, too. Then they ransacked the house."

Mom glanced at the closed cellar door. "The real estate agent told us Mrs. Donaldson died falling down the steps," she said. "But she didn't say anything about murder."

"Mrs. DiSilvio didn't tell you an out-and-out lie," Arthur said with a shrug. "She just left out a few details."

"I'm disappointed in her," Mom said. "Rhoda and I—"

"I warned you not to think of that woman as a friend," Dad interrupted. "Rhoda's a real estate agent. She wanted to sell us the house, pure and simple."

"Well, if she'd told us the whole truth, I wouldn't have bought the place," Mom said.

"And that's exactly why she didn't." Dad picked up the empty pizza box and headed toward the kitchen. "Let's get cleaned up. We've had a big day, and I for one would like to go to bed early."

"Did they catch the killer?" Mom asked Arthur.

He shook his head. "Grandma thinks he's still in town. Most likely he'll strike again. You know, like those serial killers you hear about."

Just then the shrill sound of a police whistle shattered the evening. Mom gasped in alarm, and I choked on a mouthful of cake.

"Don't worry," Arthur said. "That's Grandma calling me. Gotta go."

At the kitchen door, he turned and grinned at me. "I'll show you the sights tomorrow. Which will take about one minute. Then we can go to the library."

As soon as the screen door slammed shut, Mom and Dad looked at me as if I'd invented Arthur to make their lives miserable. "It's not my fault," I said. "He was lying in wait for me."

Later that night as I was getting ready for bed, I found myself hoping Arthur was right about the termites. The sooner the house fell down, the sooner we'd move to a nice house in Fair Oaks where no one had been murdered. I'd leave Arthur behind and make new friends. Just because I'd been a nerd in Richmond didn't mean I had to be a nerd here. I could start over, learn some sports, get better-looking clothes, and say the right thing instead of something dumb.

3

The next morning, Arthur walked into the kitchen while I was eating breakfast. Without waiting for an invitation, he dipped his hand into the Raisin Bran box and scooped out a helping. I watched him dump the cereal into his mouth and chew it up. "Would you like a bowl?" I asked, hoping to sound sarcastic.

"No, I already had breakfast. We get the store brand of raisin bran. I was just seeing which tasted better."

"And?"

"I like the store brand," Arthur said. "It's a better buy, too."

Mom took a break from unpacking to poke her head into the kitchen. "Good morning, Arthur. Did you tell your grandmother how much we enjoyed the cake?"

He nodded. "She was tickled pink," he said with a crooked grin. "I bet you never guessed she bought that cake at the day-old bake shop."

Mom and I looked at each other. It was true. We hadn't guessed.

"Well," Mom said, returning Arthur's grin. "I'll have to

ask your grandmother where that shop is. The next time I need cake . . ."

"It's in the shopping center on Route 23," Arthur said. "Right next to the adult video place."

Mom ignored the part about the video store. "What are you two planning to do today?"

I groaned silently. We'd been here less than twenty-four hours, and Mom was already referring to Arthur and me as "you two."

"I'm going to show Logan the town," Arthur said, scooping up another handful of Raisin Bran. Mom ignored that, too.

"Behave yourselves," she said. "And be back in time for lunch."

I followed Arthur outside and nearly tripped over Bear, who was lying near the door. He raised his head and looked at me, then sighed and began scratching his side.

"Poor fella," Arthur said. "He really loved Mrs. Donaldson."

"I wish Mom and Dad hadn't bought this house," I said.

"Well, I'm glad they did," Arthur said. "It's nice having someone to hang out with. I don't have a lot of friends, you know."

That was no surprise, but I didn't tell him that. Even if we didn't move to Fair Oaks before school started, I'd make new friends anyway. I wasn't about to spend the rest of my life stuck with a weird kid like Arthur.

An ancient girl's three-speed Raleigh with a big straw basket attached to its handlebars leaned against the porch. I'd have rather walked than ride something that clunky. But

Arthur straddled it and grinned. "Come on," he said, "I'll show you the spectacular sights of Bealesville."

I went to the garage and wheeled out my bike, a red Trek with more gears than I knew what to do with and brakes quick enough to pitch me over the handlebars. Dad had bought new bikes for all three of us. Now that we were living near the mountains, he planned for us to do a lot of riding on park trails.

"That sure is one fancy bike. But you know what?" Arthur patted the Raleigh's handlebars. "This is the best bike ever made. It's a genuine classic."

Dad came to the kitchen door. "Don't forget your helmet, Logan!" He tossed it to me from the back porch.

Arthur watched me fasten the strap under my chin. "Do you have fancy spandex shorts, too?" he asked. "And special shoes that snap to the pedals?"

I shook my head, irritated by the sarcastic edge to his questions. "Where's your helmet?" I asked.

"Grandma says helmets take all the fun out of bike riding."

"If you're under eighteen, you have to wear one. It's the law."

Arthur shrugged. "Grandma says the cops have more important things to do than arrest kids for not wearing helmets."

"Your grandmother sure has a lot of opinions."

"You can say that again." Arthur pushed off and wobbled down the driveway toward the street. If any kid needed protection, he did.

"Hey," I called. "I bet Dad can lend you a helmet."

Arthur shook his head. "I don't need it."

I followed him down the shady street, glad to see he was doing better now that he was pedaling faster.

True to his word, it didn't take long to tour Bealesville proper. We cruised up and down a few hilly streets. Arthur pointed out various houses. The police chief lived in a brick rambler at the end of Albert Street. The principal of the middle school lived in a huge Victorian at the top of the hill on Magruder Road. A doctor lived in another mansion across the way. A dentist was close by in a tidy brick colonial on Sheraton Street. His fence was made of a row of wooden teeth, complete with a sign that said, TOOTH ACRE. I hoped he wasn't the only dentist in town.

"How come so many houses have those signs in their yards?" I pointed to a bunch sprouting like mushrooms on the dentist's lawn. One said, SAVE THE MAGIC. Another said, SAY NO TO CHESTNUT MANOR ESTATES.

Arthur screwed up his face in disgust. "Lots of people want to save the old amusement park out on Route 23—the Magic Forest, it was called. After it closed, some corporation bought the land. Got it cheap, according to Grandma. They plan to tear down what's left of the place and build a big development there—more huge houses like the ones in Fair Oaks, plus an outlet mall, a bunch of restaurants, and a multiplex movie theater."

"That doesn't sound so bad."

Arthur shrugged. "People here like things the way they are. They don't want Bealesville to become a suburb of Richmond."

Maneuvering around a parked car, he added, "The Magic

Forest is a really neat place. It's all grown over with vines and stuff, and the rides and buildings are falling down. Somebody could film a great horror movie there."

With that, Arthur pedaled down Tulip Road, picking up speed as he coasted to Main Street at the bottom of the hill. The biggest house was Bradley's Funeral Home, which had provided fine service for seventy-five years, according to the sign in the front yard. Next to Bradley's establishment was the Quiet Hours Nursing Home, which I guessed was a convenient arrangement, considering that the cemetery was directly across the street. Some old folks were sitting in rockers on the front porch gazing at the green grass and marble headstones. Maybe that's what you did when you were their age—contemplated your eternal resting place. Maybe it helped you get used to the idea of dying. But I doubted it.

"That's where Mrs. Donaldson's funeral was." Arthur pointed to Bradley's. "Lots of people came—so many they had to get in line and wait to go in. Fire laws, you know." He swerved to avoid hitting a fire hydrant he hadn't noticed.

"Most of them didn't even know her," he went on, as if he hadn't just missed fracturing his skull. "They went because she was murdered."

"Did you go?"

"Of course. She was a nice old lady." He paused to watch a dog dash across the street in pursuit of a cat.

I looked at Arthur with admiration, maybe even envy. I'd never been to a funeral. Not even my grandparents' or my favorite aunt's. Mom thought I was too young to be exposed to such things, but I felt as if I'd missed out on something. Every kid I knew had been to at least one funeral.

"Let's get moving." Arthur took off down another steep hill, and I pedaled after him, hoping to see the rest of the town before he killed himself in a spectacular bike crash.

On Main Street, we passed a bunch of truly boring stores—an insurance agency, an office-supply store, and Mrs. DiSilvio's real estate office, its windows plastered with photos of houses. It was the only business that didn't have a SAVE THE MAGIC sign in its window.

Across the street was a drugstore, Golden Joe's Pizza Go-Go, and three or four consignment shops, selling everything from old clothes to even older appliances. The whole street had a tired look.

"Everybody goes to Wal-Mart now," Arthur explained. "Grandma says it's a real pity. She used to work in a nice little card shop, but it closed last year. People can buy stuff cheaper at Wal-Mart."

I'd heard my parents complain about the same thing. Dad was still mad about some big hardware chain that drove his favorite store out of business. But I guessed that's how it was. People went where they got the best prices. You couldn't really blame them.

At last Arthur stopped in front of the library, a tiny little store-front branch not even a third the size of the one back home. Its windows were plastered with SAVE THE MAGIC signs.

"I thought you might want to get a library card," he said, dumping his classic Raleigh on the sidewalk.

I locked my Trek to a bike rack, took off my helmet, and followed him inside, glad to escape the heat. The librarian sitting at the information desk smiled at Arthur. "Well, well," she said, "here's my favorite customer. Who's this with you?"

"Logan Forbes," Arthur said. "He just moved into Mrs. Donaldson's house. Right next door to me."

"Oh, yes, I heard the new art teacher bought the place." She turned her smile on me. "I'm Mrs. Bailey, Logan. Are you a bookworm like my buddy Arthur?"

I shrugged. Here was another person linking me with Arthur. It seemed there was no escaping it—I was doomed to be Arthur's friend.

"Reading's okay," I said as I took the pen she offered me and filled out an application for a library card. Like Arthur, I'd been the prize winner in my school's read-a-thon, but I didn't want people thinking we were just alike. If I hadn't been scared of being caught in a lie, I'd have said I was too busy playing sports to read. That would have set us apart. Arthur was obviously no better at physical stuff than I was.

"We'll get your card into the mail tomorrow or the day after," she promised. "In the meantime, Arthur can let you check out some books on his card."

"Sure," Arthur said, "as long as you bring them back on time. I've never had an overdue in my life."

Mrs. Bailey laughed. "Arthur is absolutely exemplary in that regard."

"Come on," Arthur said to me. "I'll give you a tour."

We went to the children's room first, a small area in the back. I could tell at a glance I'd read most of the books.

"You can order stuff from other libraries," Arthur said as if he'd guessed what I was thinking. "That's how I read so many last year. I'm not sure there are even 500 books in this whole library."

We browsed around a while. In the teen section, I found a science fiction paperback that looked good. Arthur picked up *The Shining* and started flipping through it.

"Hey, I've got an idea," he said. "Let's get the newspaper from the day Mrs. Donaldson was killed so you can read all about it."

Without waiting for a response, Arthur headed back to Mrs. Bailey's desk. "Do you remember when Mrs. Donaldson was murdered?"

Mrs. Bailey thought a minute or two. "Three years ago, July seventeenth. I remember because I was baking my daughter's birthday cake. I'd just counted out six candles when I heard the announcement on the radio."

"Could we see the newspaper from that day?" Arthur asked. "Logan wants to know everything about it, since it happened in his house and all."

"I'll be right back." Mrs. Bailey opened a door marked STAFF ONLY and went inside.

"I don't want to read about it," I muttered.

"Yes, you do," Arthur said.

I shrugged. Actually, he was right. I couldn't help being curious. But I didn't want to admit it. Wasn't it kind of morbid?

"Here it is." Mrs. Bailey had reappeared, holding a big book. "These are the 2006 *Bealesville Posts,* all bound together in chronological order."

Arthur led the way to a reading table and put the book down, turning the pages quickly to find what he wanted. Each time a page turned, motes of dust flew up and tickled my nose.

"*Voilà!*" Arthur pointed a grubby finger at a front-page headline, dated July 17.

MYRTLE E. DONALDSON MURDERED IN HER HOME

BEALESVILLE. "Things like this don't happen in Bealesville," Evan McEwan said when he learned of Mrs. Donaldson's murder.

Unfortunately, Mr. McEwan is wrong. Like our big-city cousins, our small town has its own murder to deal with, and everyone is reeling in shock, including the police, who have no leads as to the killer's identity.

NEIGHBOR DISCOVERS BODY

Yesterday, Darla Jenkins, age 68, of 4301 Navajo Street found her neighbor dead at the bottom of the cellar steps. Myrtle E. Donaldson, age 61, died from head injuries resulting from the fall. The house was in disarray, leading police to theorize that Mrs. Donaldson was the victim of a robbery. She was apparently pushed down the steps by an intruder who also tried, but failed, to kill her dog.

So far the police have no suspects.

WILL BE REMEMBERED BY MANY

Mrs. Donaldson will be remembered by many as the genial ticket taker at the beloved Magic Forest Amusement Park on Route 23 West. She was employed there from 1960 until her untimely death.

The only blot on her career was the recent discovery that a large sum of money had been embezzled from the park. Mrs. Donaldson was questioned more than once, leading some to believe she was the chief suspect, but no evidence was found linking her to the crime.

The theft forced the park's owner, Edward Farrell, into bankruptcy. Consequently, he has no plans to reopen next summer. In fact, he has already received an offer from someone interested in developing the land.

Thus ends a tradition of cooling off with Old King Cole, Willie the Blue Whale, Cinderella, and all the other beloved, larger-than-life nursery rhyme characters.

POLICE CHIEF AT A LOSS

In his statement to the press regarding Mrs. Donaldson's death, police chief Robert Manning refuted allegations of a connection between the murder and the amusement park's missing funds. He has requested that anyone with information about the murder step forward.

At this time, Chief Manning believes Mrs. Donaldson was the victim of a random killing committed by a stranger passing through Bealesville in search of money or valuables.

We hope this proves to be correct and not the beginning of a crime wave in our peaceful town.

FUNERAL

Services for Myrtle E. Donaldson will be held at Bradley's Funeral Home on July 22nd at ten a.m. Burial will follow at Still Waters Memorial Gardens.

Mrs. Donaldson, a lifelong resident of Bealesville, was predeceased by her parents, Daniel and Sophie Atkins, and her husband, Peter Donaldson. She leaves her daughter, Violet Phelps; her son-in-law, Silas Phelps; two grandchildren, several nieces and nephews, and numerous friends and relatives.

I studied Mrs. Donaldson's smiling photograph. She wasn't the sort of person you'd expect to end up getting murdered in her own home. Or to be suspected of embezzling. "Do you think she stole the money?" I asked.

"No way." Arthur touched Mrs. Donaldson's photograph with his stubby finger. "But you know how it is. People started rumors, and pretty soon most of the town believed she'd hidden it somewhere in her house—which could be why Silas Phelps killed her."

"Silas Phelps?" I stared at Arthur. "The newspaper said the police had no suspects."

Arthur shrugged. "Grandma is positive he did it."

"But he was her son-in-law—"

"If you'd lived in Bealesville as long as I have," Arthur said, "you'd understand. The Phelpses and the Jarmons are the worst families in town. They're all related to each other—the most twisted DNA you'll ever come across. Grandma says they're directly descended from Cain."

Arthur leaned closer. "Silas is the worst of all the Phelps. You could call him a one-man crime wave. Car theft, armed robbery, drugs, assault—he's been in jail most of his adult life."

Noticing I'd gotten kind of tense, Arthur patted my shoulder. "You don't have to worry about Silas. He's back in jail for holding up a gas station out on Route 703. Used a gun. . . . He's one bad dude."

While I sat there picturing Silas as a modern-day Bill Sykes straight out of *Oliver Twist,* Arthur turned to the next day's paper. For about a week, the murder was covered, slowly working its way from front-page headlines to back-page paragraphs, tucked away between bicycle thefts and other small-town stuff. But it was always the same. Except for the occasional mention of the embezzled money, there was no clue to who killed Mrs. Donaldson—or why.

"Well, that's it." Arthur got up and stretched, inflating his bony chest with a deep breath. "You want to make some photocopies for your parents? They should know the facts."

I reached into my pocket. Four quarters, two nickels, and three pennies: more than enough to copy the first article, which was the most important one. And, as Arthur pointed out, the only one that mentioned his grandmother.

"Make me a copy, too," Arthur said. "I'll pay you back."

I doubted that, but I made him a copy anyway. Arthur carried the heavy book back to Mrs. Bailey. She took it and handed it to a woman standing beside her.

"Here you are," she said. "It's so odd to have two people wanting the same year of the *Bealesville Post* on the same day."

The woman smiled at Arthur and me. Even though she was at least thirty, she was still really good looking. Long dark hair, pretty eyes, nice mouth, small nose. Kind of tall, slim but not skinny—she was built, really built. Arthur and I ogled her shamelessly.

"Why would boys your age be reading musty old newspapers?" she asked in a friendly way.

Arthur gestured at me and said, "My friend Logan just moved into the house next door to me. An old lady got killed there three years ago. He wanted to see the newspaper story."

He held up his photocopy, which was already creased and

dirty, and the lady leaned down to take a look. Her long hair swung against Arthur's cheek, and he blushed.

"What an amazing coincidence," she said. "That's the very story I'm looking for."

"How come?" Arthur asked, obviously puzzled.

"I'm an investigative reporter from the *Richmond Times*," she said. "We're running a series on unsolved crimes, what they call 'cold case files.' My editor assigned the Donaldson killing to me."

"You should talk to my grandmother," Arthur said. "She's the one who found the body. See?" He stabbed at his photocopy with his finger. "That's her. Mrs. Darla Jenkins. My name's Arthur. We live right next door to Mrs. Donaldson's old house, where Logan's living now."

The woman opened her purse and pulled out a notebook. "Please give me your grandmother's name and phone number. I'll call her."

"D-a-r-l-a J-e-n-k-i-n-s," Arthur spelled, even though the woman probably already knew how to spell both names. "Our phone number is unlisted." Lowering his voice, he whispered the number.

She wrote it down carefully. "Thank you, Arthur." Turning to me, she added, "If it's all right with your parents, I'd like to see your house and take some photographs. May I have your parents' names and phone number, too?"

I gave them to her, and she thanked us again. "My name is Nina Stevens." She handed us each a small white card with her name and phone number on it. "Now, I must read these articles. It was nice meeting you. I'll see you soon."

With that, she sat down and began poring over the newspaper.

Outside, the sun hit my face like a blast from a furnace. I wished I hadn't spent my money on photocopies. An ice-cold soda sure would've tasted good.

"We might get in the newspaper, Logan," Arthur said happily. "Maybe she'll even take our pictures. Won't that be something to talk about when school starts?"

I nodded, but I didn't see why Nina Stevens would want to waste her time photographing us. There was no sense telling Arthur that, though. Let him daydream about being famous, if it made him happy.

5

When I got home, the first thing I saw was Johnny O'Neil mowing the lawn. He was riding one of those little tractor things, and grass flew everywhere. It smelled like summer, sweet and fresh and damp.

Mom was sitting on the front porch reading a crime novel. I dropped the photocopy in her lap. "Want to read about a *real* murder?"

She jumped as if I'd dropped the body itself in her lap, but she read the article. When she finished, she looked up at me. "I'd almost convinced myself Arthur made the whole thing up, but I guess it's true after all." She shivered and folded her arms tightly across her chest. "That poor woman. Such a horrible way to die."

I sat down beside her. "When Arthur and I were at the library, we met a reporter from the *Richmond Times*. Her paper's doing a series on unsolved crimes—you know, what they call 'cold case files.' She's writing about Mrs. Donaldson's murder, and she wants to take some pictures of our house."

"I'd better tell your father." Photocopy in hand, Mom went inside, with me right behind her. Dad was in the kitchen, talking to a contractor about a new roof.

"Look at this." Mom waved the photocopy. "Everything Arthur said is true. Mrs. Donaldson really was murdered right here in this very room."

The contractor nodded affably. "Didn't you folks know that?"

Mom shook her head. "Isn't there some sort of law that makes it illegal to hide things like this about a house?" she asked.

Dad sighed. "It's hardly worth pursuing. We've bought the place, we've moved in, I've hired a roofer, a plumber, and an electrician. I can't see leaving because a woman was murdered here."

"I'll never enjoy cooking a meal in this kitchen," Mom said.

Dad gave her a long look. "Let's face it, Carolyn. You've never enjoyed cooking a meal anywhere."

The contractor and I laughed, but Mom poured herself a cup of coffee and went outside to drink it on the porch. She'd never had much of a sense of humor about herself.

That evening, Nina Stevens called and made a date to come to our house the very next day. So when Arthur showed up at breakfast in the morning, I stopped him in the doorway. "Guess who's coming at eleven o'clock to take pictures of the crime scene?"

"She'll be at my house at ten sharp to talk to Grandma."

Arthur slipped past me and helped himself to a glass of orange juice.

"She's taking pictures of Grandma and me, too." He scooped up his usual handful of Raisin Bran and stuffed it in his mouth. "What do you want to do till she gets here?"

"Finish my breakfast," I said.

Arthur laughed and took a second helping of Raisin Bran.

At nine thirty, we perched on Arthur's front steps and played chess while we waited for Miss Stevens. Much as I hated to admit it, Arthur was better at strategy than I was. By the time a sporty little red Miata pulled into the driveway, I was losing big-time.

Scattering chessmen everywhere, we jumped to our feet, waving like loyal subjects. If I'd had a cap, I would've doffed it.

"Good morning, Miss Stevens," Arthur said, giving her his biggest grin. "Welcome to our humble abode!"

She smiled. "'Miss Stevens' sounds so formal. Why don't you boys just call me Nina?"

"Nina." Arthur drew in his breath as he'd just said a magic word. "All right, Nina!"

Mrs. Jenkins must have been looking out the window, for she joined us on the porch before Nina had reached the first step.

After she'd introduced herself, Nina complimented Mrs. Jenkins on the blossoms of a scraggly rose bush languishing by the porch.

Mrs. Jenkins laughed. "That poor old bush has seen better days—just like me."

Arthur and I followed the women inside. If I hadn't been

so eager to hear every word Nina said, I'd have probably been more amazed by Mrs. Jenkins's decorating taste: one wall tiled with mirrors, a huge recliner in front of the TV, a sagging sofa with faded slipcovers, a lava lamp on a small table, and at least a dozen badly done paintings of clowns on the walls, plus crowds of little ceramic clowns on the mantelpiece, on knickknack shelves, on top of the TV, and surrounding the lava lamp.

"She collects them," Arthur whispered. "Don't ask me why."

In the kitchen—where more clowns leered at us from the walls and countertops—Nina sat down at the table and opened a little notebook.

Before she asked about Mrs. Donaldson, she said, "I just love your clowns, Mrs. Jenkins. They're adorable. You must have been collecting them for years."

Mrs. Jenkins looked around the room. "You know how it is," she said with a smile. "You get a few here and a few there. Before you know it, people start giving them to you. Pretty soon you have more than you know what to do with." She picked up one and grinned at its round face. "You can never have enough clowns."

At last, Nina began asking Mrs. Jenkins about Mrs. Donaldson. She seemed especially interested in the Magic Forest. "Do you think she embezzled the money?"

"No, indeed!" Mrs. Jenkins glared at Nina. "Myrtle Donaldson was the most honest woman in the world. I never heard her tell a lie or cheat in any way. It hurt her deeply to be questioned about the missing money."

Nina paused and jotted down a few words in her notebook. "People who know the victims often think they know who killed them," she said. "I was wondering if you—"

"I'd put my money on Silas Phelps." Mrs. Jenkins sat up straighter. "There was bad blood between him and Myrtle. She didn't want him to marry her daughter, Violet. Did her best to prevent it. But Violet ran off and married him anyway."

She took a swallow of coffee. "Silas treated that poor girl real bad. She was always coming home to her mother, dragging her kids with her. Then Silas would show up, demanding she come home, and he and Myrtle would get into it. I had to call the police more than once. I was scared he'd kill all of them. You read about things like that in the paper—but I guess in your profession you know that."

When Mrs. Jenkins paused to wave a fly away from the sugar bowl, Nina said, "But why would he kill her? What was his motive?"

"Here's what I think." Mrs. Jenkins looked at all of us as if to make sure we were listening. "Silas probably believed Myrtle had the missing money hidden in her house. He came to get it, and when she put up a fight, he killed her. As I said, he never liked her. Or the dog."

"Why do you think the police didn't suspect Silas?"

"Oh, they talked to him, but he said he was home watching TV, and Violet backed him up. She was so scared of him, she'd say whatever he told her to say—even with her hand on the Bible. She was more scared of Silas than the Lord, and that's the sad truth of it."

Mrs. Jenkins pressed her lips together and shook her head sadly. "I still miss Myrtle. You never get over a murder, especially when the killer's out there somewhere, free to do what he likes, and Myrtle's dead in her grave."

"Silas is in jail now," Arthur pointed out.

"But not for murder," Mrs. Jenkins said. "He'll be out in no time—just you wait and see."

"What became of Violet?" Nina asked.

Mrs. Jenkins poured herself another cup of coffee. "She and the kids are living in a mobile home out at the Phelps place. Can't afford to move." She thought a moment. "The last I heard, Violet was working at the Wal-Mart on Route 23. She might still be there—not many jobs in Bealesville."

"Thanks, I'll see if I can find her." Nina jotted something in her notebook. "There's one other thing you could probably help me with. I rented a car, but it doesn't have a navigational device. With my terrible sense of direction, I'm thinking of hiring a local to show me the area."

"Me!" Arthur jumped up as if he were volunteering for extra credit at school. "I can show you everything in Bealesville and beyond. Ask Logan—I just gave him a great tour."

Nina smiled. "Thanks, Arthur, but I want someone who's at least eighteen."

"Try Johnny O'Neil at Golden Joe's Pizza Go-Go," Mrs. Jenkins suggested. "He's always looking for extra cash."

Nina wrote down Johnny's name and closed her notebook. "Now, if I could take a few pictures, I'll be on my way. I've taken up far too much of your time already."

It was what Arthur and I had been waiting for. Flanking

Mrs. Jenkins, we grinned through at least ten shots. After Nina took some of Mrs. Jenkins by herself, she went outside and aimed her camera at our house. She must have shot dozens of pictures from all possible angles.

Nina noticed Bear sitting on our back porch. "Is that your dog, Logan?"

"No," Arthur said, without giving me a chance to do more than open my mouth. "That's Bear, Mrs. Donaldson's dog. Grandma and I have been taking care of him since she was killed, but he spends most of his time on Logan's porch. I think he's waiting for Mrs. Donaldson to come home."

"How sad." Nina followed Arthur and me into my yard and took a few pictures of Bear lying by our door.

Mom and Dad stepped outside to welcome Nina. Inside, she devoted herself to photographing every room upstairs and down, including the dark, cobwebby basement. She wanted a feeling, she said, of Mrs. Donaldson's life—and death.

"Does that lead to the attic?" she asked, pointing to a door in the upstairs hall.

"Yep," Dad said. "I'm planning to have a fan installed to draw the hot air out of the house. It'll be a very efficient cooling system."

"Is it possible for me to have a look?"

"Of course." He opened the door to a steep flight of steps leading up into dusty darkness. "Nothing to see," he said. "Just dust and a ton of Mrs. Donaldson's junk that nobody ever removed."

Nina climbed the stairs and disappeared into the darkness. She stayed there so long I was tempted to ask if she was okay, When she finally came down, she had a smudge of dirt on her cheek and cobwebs in her hair.

"Well," she said, "if you could tell me a little bit about why you moved to Bealesville and how you felt when you learned Mrs. Donaldson was murdered, I'll be finished here."

"I got a job at the high school, teaching art," Dad began.

"And we were sick of the crime in Richmond," Mom put in. "So what happens? We buy a house in a small town and find out the previous owner was murdered."

Nina looked sympathetic. "You must have been horrified."

Mom nodded, but before she could elaborate, Nina got up to leave. "Thank you so much for your time."

"When will the story be in the paper?" Arthur asked her.

"I'm not sure," she said. "It's part of a series. I suppose the editors will decide when all the articles are ready."

Arthur and I followed Nina outside and watched her drive away in her nifty red car.

"You know what we should do?" Arthur said. "Ride our bikes to the Magic Forest and take a look around. I haven't been out there for ages."

"I thought you said it was closed."

"It is." Arthur picked up a stone and chucked it at a pot drooping with dead flowers on his back porch. The stone thunked against the house, missing the pot by at least a foot. "But I know how to get in. You ought to see it before it's bull-dozed."

"Logan," Mom called, "lunch will be ready soon."

Arthur was about to follow me, but his grandmother stopped him. "There's a nice bologna sandwich waiting for you on the table, Artie."

"See you later," he called and ran inside.

6

Arthur showed up after lunch, just in time to wolf down at least half a bag of fancy chocolate-chip cookies—the expensive kind Mom usually doles out two at a time.

"I guess I'd have to say these are better than the grocery-store brand Grandma buys," he admitted.

As he reached for another helping, Mom snatched up the bag and put it in the cupboard, slamming the door a little more forcefully than necessary.

"Let's go outside," I said, hoping to preserve the peace. Although Arthur didn't realize it, he was perilously close to being sent home in disgrace.

Unaware that he'd done anything wrong, Arthur followed me onto the back porch. "How about riding our bikes to the Magic Forest?" he asked.

"How far is it?"

Arthur shrugged. "A couple of miles, I guess."

We pedaled down Navajo Street to Route 23 West. As we neared the Toot 'n' Tote convenience store on the edge of town, five boys about my age came outside carrying big cups of soda. The minute they spotted Arthur, they surrounded his bike and mine.

"Hey, it's Art the fart," a lanky redhead said.

A mean-faced kid wearing a faded T-shirt grabbed Arthur's handlebars. "Cool bike," he said. "Where did you find it? At the junkyard?"

"Remove your filthy hands from my bicycle," Arthur said in what could only be described as a snooty voice.

"Who's going to make me?" Mean Face asked, looking even meaner—if that was possible.

Then the redhead noticed me. "Hey, look. Arthur's got a friend."

The boys lost interest in Arthur. "What's your name?" Mean Face asked me. "Where do you live?"

"His name's Logan," Arthur answered for me, which was just as well because my mouth had gone dry. "He lives right next door to me."

"You live in my grandma's house?" Mean Face dropped his voice a few notches lower. His face was so close to mine, I could see the pores in his skin. And the anger in his eyes. "She was murdered there," he added in an even lower voice, almost a hiss. "Did you know that?"

From the look on his face, you'd think *I'd* killed his grandmother. "Arthur told me," I managed to say in a sort of squeaky voice.

"Arthur told him." Mean Face turned to his friends and laughed. "Arthur the idiot told him. Arthur the moron told him."

They took it up like a chant. The words ran together, losing their meaning, making my head hurt. *"Arthurtoldhim, Arthurtoldhim, Arthurtoldhim. Arthurtheidiot, Arthurthemoron."*

While they chanted, they tried to yank my bike away. One cuffed my helmet. Another snatched my water bottle. Just as I toppled off my bike, somebody grabbed Mean Face and gave him a shake.

"Hey, what do you think you're doing, Danny?"

It was Johnny O'Neil. The other boys backed away.

"Nothing," Mean Face muttered.

"Just kidding around," the redheaded kid added. "That's all."

"Imbeciles." Arthur spoke just loud enough for the boys to hear. Very smart, I thought, definite proof he was a true genius.

"You okay, Logan?" Johnny asked.

"Yeah, sure." I got to my feet and straightened my helmet, picked up my bike, and stuck the water bottle in its holder. My left knee was scraped and bleeding, but I didn't mention it.

The boys lingered in a tight little gang, watching us, ready to run if they had to.

"Have you started working for Nina yet?" Arthur asked Johnny.

Johnny glanced at Arthur. "Who?"

"Nina Stevens," Arthur said, "the reporter from Richmond, the one who's working on Mrs. Donaldson's murder."

"Oh, yeah, Nina the reporter. Good-looking lady." He tossed a strand of dark hair out of his eyes and grinned. "Couldn't do it—I'm working two jobs already, delivering pizza and helping Logan's dad. I gave her Billy Jarmon's number. He's always looking for work."

"You gave that bum Nina's phone number?" Arthur stared at him in disbelief.

Johnny tapped Arthur's bony chest with one finger, just hard enough to hurt. "Hey, kid, watch what you say about Billy. He's my cousin, you know."

Arthur backed away and straddled his bike. "Come on, Logan," he muttered.

Johnny gave my shoulder a playful punch and headed into the convenience store. "Tell your dad I'll be by this afternoon to finish the lawn," he called from the door.

Mean-Face Danny and his gang had regrouped under a tree at the edge of the Toot 'n' Tote parking lot. The redhead gave me the finger, but I pretended not to see. Arthur was already several yards ahead, pumping hard, and I pedaled after him. Since the boys didn't have bikes, they couldn't follow us. A big relief.

"Danny Phelps is my number-one enemy," Arthur said. "He hates me because I'm smarter than him and all his family put together. He's the dumbest kid in Bealesville. If a teacher could stand him for more than one year, he'd be lucky to be in second grade."

"Why did he say I live in his grandmother's house?"

"Because you do. Violet's his mother, and Silas is his old man." Arthur turned his head to grin at me and almost rode off the road. Swerving away from a ditch, he added, "Danny was nicer before his grandma was murdered. In fact, he was almost human. Believe it or not, we used to play together when he was staying at your house—you know, those times when Violet had to get away from Silas." Arthur frowned. "Of course, we were little then. By grade school, I had figured out he was a dope."

Out of town, Route 23 turned into a narrow highway with more curves and hills than a roller coaster. Trucks and cars whizzed past as I struggled uphill and wobbled down, braking to keep from going too fast. I couldn't understand how Arthur managed to get ahead of me on a three-speed bike.

Worse yet, the road's shoulder was narrow, overgrown with weeds, and littered with stuff thrown from car windows—beer and soda cans, bottles, plastic bags, fast-food wrappings. We had to ride on the edge of the asphalt most of the time.

Houses got farther apart, and soon we were in farm country. Rolling hills stretched away toward the mountains. Cows lay in the shade, chewing their cuds, looking thoughtful. Now and then a dog barked. The air smelled of honeysuckle and cut grass and diesel fumes. If it hadn't been for the hills and the traffic and the heat, it would have been a great ride.

After an hour or more, we reached the top of a hill. Below us I saw a fake stone castle wall with towers. Near the road, a life-size statue of Old King Cole perched on top of a tall sign that said, WELCOME TO THE MAGIC FOREST. The statue's paint was faded, his body was cracked, and he was missing an arm. The other arm pointed at a sagging red gate. Over it, a tilting green dragon, minus a tail, stood guard, grinning a goofy grin. On the gate, a sign riddled with bullet holes said, CLOSED FOR THE SEASON. Arthur sped down the hill, holding both skinny arms above his head, something I didn't dare do, and yelling, "Wahooo!"

"Are you crazy?" I hollered, but he was already at the bottom, screeching to a stop in the weedy parking lot.

The gate to the park was padlocked, but Arthur led me to a narrow path running along a sagging chain-link fence posted with NO TRESPASSING signs and red notices warning that the property was condemned as unsafe.

Hiding our bikes in the bushes, we followed the fence into the woods, trying to see what was on the other side. It was no use. A wild green vine draped everything—the fence, trees, telephone poles.

"It's a jungle," I said.

"Kudzu," Arthur said. "It grows all over everything." Warming to the subject, he elaborated. "Kudzu, the killer plant! Engulfs entire buildings, towns, trains, cars. It's unstoppable, indestructible, determined to conquer the world. Soon—"

"Stop!" I gave Arthur a shove, and he staggered backward, giggling.

"It's true," he said. "Once it gets started, kudzu takes over. Grandma knew this man who never left his house, too lazy to do anything but lie around all day. Well, one day he decided he just had to go to the store, but when he opened his door, all he saw was kudzu. He didn't have a hatchet or a chain saw so he was trapped. Pretty soon the kudzu oozed in under the door and through the windows. Now you'd never know a house was there."

"What happened to the man?"

Arthur shrugged. "I guess he's still in there."

"That's not true," I said, annoyed at myself for almost believing him.

"Ask Grandma. You didn't believe me about the murder, either."

I followed him deeper into the jungle. At last we came to a gap in the fence just big enough for us to squeeze through. Another bullet-ridden NO TRESPASSING sign hung over our heads. Arthur wiggled through the hole anyway.

"How about the sign?" I pointed at the red words printed on a rusty white background.

He shrugged. "I've ridden my bike out here lots of times, and I've never seen a watchman or a guard dog or anything—except maybe some teenagers fooling around. It's a great place to pretend you're searching for the ruins of ancient civilizations. Like Indiana Jones in the movies."

I hesitated, but Arthur was already vanishing into the kudzu. Taking a deep breath, I followed him into the Magic Forest. It was the first time I'd ever trespassed, and I couldn't help thinking I'd just taken a step into a new—and dangerous—life.

7

Arthur led me down an overgrown path, stopping now and then to examine a crumbling building or the remains of a ride. Here and there, storybook figures emerged from the kudzu, lopsided, grotesque, their noses gone, their fingers missing, their skin leprous with moss and mold. The place was a nightmare version of Mother Goose.

"Do you read *Zippy the Pinhead*?" Arthur asked. "The comic strip?"

I shook my head, too amazed by my surroundings to be interested in anything else.

"Zippy's this guy with a pointed head and a little topknot tied with a bow. He wears a long robe and he loves talking to giant sculptures, the kind that advertise things like restaurants and ice-cream stands and car-repair shops."

I glanced at Arthur. "Yeah?"

"In one strip, Zippy came here once and talked to some of them." Arthur waved his arm at the crumbling statues.

"Now that I think about it, Dad loves Zippy," I said, "but I always thought he was kind of boring."

"You just don't get the humor." Arthur's tone of voice suggested I might not be smart enough to appreciate Zippy. "It's very erudite. Which means—"

"I know what it means," I interrupted. "I'm just as smart as you are. I just don't like Zippy, that's all."

Arthur shrugged and kept walking. In a few minutes we came to a pond scummed so thick with algae it looked as if you could walk on it without getting your feet wet. Across a little bridge was a big blue whale made of fiberglass, chipped and worn from years of snow and sleet and rain. Kids had spray painted him all over with graffiti and gang tags.

"It's Willie the Whale." Arthur led the way across the bridge and knelt down beside the old hulk. Pushing some vines aside, he crawled into the whale's huge open mouth.

"Grandma took a picture of me in here." He struck a silly pose and grinned. "I wore a paper crown—they gave you one when you bought a ticket. I was King Arthur—get it?"

The whale smelled damp and mildewy, like an old basement with no windows. Spiderwebs hung from the roof of Willie's mouth, filled with little mummified insects. Beetles scurried away into the dark. Slugs had left slimy trails everywhere.

"This is disgusting," I told Arthur.

"It was fun when I was little." He picked at a red flake of paint on Willie's tongue.

"Shh!" I grabbed his arm. "Somebody's coming!"

Without a word, the two of us pressed ourselves against the back of Willie's mouth, somewhere near his tonsils. Images of drug dealers and dangerous criminals flitted across the little movie screen in my head. Here we were, miles from help. No one knew where we were. Mom had warned me about lonely places. Why hadn't I listened?

Soon two people appeared. One was Nina. Wearing tan shorts and a plain white T-shirt, her expensive camera hanging from a shoulder strap, she looked as classy as ever.

The man with her was in his twenties, maybe younger. His dark glasses made it hard to tell. He wore faded jeans with one knee ripped out. His arms were tattooed from wrist to shoulder, and his hair was cut so short I could see his scalp. Next to him, Johnny looked like the All-American boy.

"It's Billy Jarmon," Arthur whispered. "Nina must have taken Johnny's advice and asked him to show her the sights." He shook his head in disgust. "She should've hired me."

"He looks mean," I said.

Arthur nodded. "He's already been in jail at least twice. Once for breaking and entering and once for stealing a Humvee and tearing up the Magic Forest with it. Knocked down a bunch of buildings and things just for the heck of it."

Billy and Nina stopped on the bridge, a few feet away from our hiding place. While he tossed stones at beer cans floating in the gunky water, she leaned against the rail and scanned the park as though she was scouting out good pictures.

"So you think it's here somewhere?" she asked Billy.

"Must be. It's not in the house. Whoever killed her trashed the whole place looking for it. The cops searched, too."

Billy sank a beer can with a stone and made the kind of explosion sound that third graders make when they play war.

"Me and Johnny were thinking of searching the house ourselves," he said. "Just in case they missed something."

Nina shot Billy a frown, and he grinned. "Just kidding. We're law-abiding citizens, me and him. We'd never do nothing wrong."

Hearing this, Arthur poked my side and snickered. "Who do you think was riding in the Humvee with Billy when he went on his little spree?" he whispered.

From the look Nina gave Billy, I had a feeling she wasn't totally convinced he was telling her the truth about his aversion to crime.

Billy lobbed another stone and sunk a beer bottle. *Kerpow!* "We didn't think anybody would *ever* buy Mrs. Donaldson's house," he said, "but then that real estate agent got a hold of it. Mrs. DiSilvio's so slick she could sell George Washington off a one-dollar bill. I guess she learned some tricks from her old man."

Nina looked at him curiously. "What do you mean?"

He spat into the pond. "Mr. DiSilvio ain't what most people think. He puts on airs and sponsors soccer teams and donates money to the library and the hospital, but you dig deep enough, you'll find he's got another side altogether."

"Maybe I should interview him."

"You won't learn nothing from that guy," Billy said. "Like I said, he's slicker than slick."

"He owns the corporation that bought this property." Nina waved a hand at the kudzu and the overgrown paths and poor old Willie, crumbling away in his scummy pond. "I hear he got it cheap."

"Nobody thought it was worth anything then. I mean, the place was broke and people were starting to go to big parks like King's Dominion. You ever been there? They got some great rides. The Rebel Yell, the Cobra." Billy threw a stone at Willie. It bounced off the fiberglass over our heads with a loud *thunk*.

Nina nodded thoughtfully and aimed her camera at the whale. "Just a few more pictures," she said, "and we can leave."

Arthur chose that moment to scoot out of Willie's mouth, straight into another photo opportunity.

"What are you kids doing here?" Billy yelled.

I was about to run, but Arthur walked right up to him. "What's it to you?"

Billy scowled, but Arthur stood his ground, arms folded, and looked him in the eye. Why was he always bent on antagonizing people who could pulverize us? First Danny and his gang. Now Billy. Was he crazy or what?

Nina stepped in front of Arthur. "I met these boys at the library," she told Billy. "Logan lives in the house where Mrs. Donaldson was murdered, and Arthur lives next door. His grandmother—"

Still scowling, Billy said, "I already know Arthur. *And* his grandmother."

"Well, then." Nina turned to me with an apologetic smile. "Logan, this is Billy Jarmon." She spoke as if we were guests at a fancy garden party, meeting at the refreshment table.

"Pleased to meet you." I offered to shake his hand the way I'd been taught, but he ignored me. So much for being a peacemaker.

"I wanted to see where Mrs. Donaldson worked," Nina told us, "but I was uneasy about coming here alone. Johnny didn't have time to show me the park, so he gave me Billy's number. It's such a fascinating place. Absolutely surreal."

While Nina talked, Billy sighed and shifted his weight from his left foot to his right foot and back again, obviously bored. "I asked you what you're doing here," he muttered to Arthur.

"You're showing Nina around, and *I'm* showing Logan around," Arthur said in a sassy voice that made me cringe.

"Just now I seen a copperhead sunning itself on the path near the gate," Billy said. "If one of them suckers bites you . . ."

"Copperheads won't bother you if you don't bother them," Arthur said in his most irritating know-it-all voice.

I tugged at his arm to shut him up. "We ought to go," I said. "It must be nearly dinnertime."

"Snakes ain't all you got to worry about," Billy went on. "Dopers hang out here. Gangs. Types you don't want to be messing with."

"Oh, Billy, please stop." Nina looked around nervously, as if she expected to see criminals lurking in the kudzu. "You're scaring *me*."

She wasn't the only one he was scaring. Thanks to Billy, the deserted park had taken on a creepy atmosphere, and I was more than ready to leave. I tugged at Arthur's arm again, harder this time. "My mother expects me home by—"

With some annoyance, Arthur shrugged my hand off his arm. "You're not scaring me," he told Billy. "I've been here lots of times, and I've never seen anything dangerous. Not once. No snakes, no gangs, just some dopers who were too stoned to notice me."

Nina stepped between Arthur and Billy. "You know what, boys? Logan's right. It's almost five o'clock. Why don't we give you a ride home?"

"We've got our bikes," I said.

"Billy has a pickup," Nina said cheerfully. "We can load the bikes in the back."

We all looked at Billy. Nina was the only one who smiled at him. "You don't mind, do you?"

Although he didn't seem at all happy about it, Billy muttered, "Yeah, sure." To Arthur and me, he said, "Don't keep me waiting. It looks like it's going to rain."

While we'd been talking, a bank of clouds had risen above the trees, covering the sun and darkening the park. A gust of wind lifted branches, turning the leaves white side out. The kudzu reared up and swayed like a monster waving long, green shaggy arms.

"We'll meet you at the front gate," Nina said.

Arthur and I plunged into the kudzu and made our way to the fence. Thunder rumbled overhead, and the wind picked up. Though I didn't think much of Mr. Billy Jarmon, I was glad we were going to have a ride home.

8

Arthur yanked his Raleigh out of its hiding place in the weeds. "Billy's a despicable ignoramus with the social presence of a flea, just like his brothers and his sisters and his aunts and his uncles and his cousins—the ones in jail and the ones on probation and the ones who haven't been caught yet."

I tugged my bike free of a clinging kudzu vine. Five more minutes and it would've been completely engulfed. "He doesn't think much of you, either."

"I doubt he likes you any better."

"Well, I wasn't the one sassing him."

"I was *provoking* him." Arthur glanced over his bony shoulder at me. "Not sassing him."

Not sure of the difference between sassing and provoking, I stared at Arthur. "Why?"

"I just told you—he's a despicable ignoramus." Arthur laughed and shoved his bike uphill toward the remains of the Magic Forest's parking lot. "Plus he was getting on my nerves."

At the edge of the parking lot, we came to a quick stop.

Nina and Billy seemed to be arguing. She gestured and he shook his head. Under the dark, towering clouds, they looked small and sort of helpless—even Billy.

"I bet Billy's mad at Nina for offering us a ride," I said.

Arthur scowled. "He'd better be nice to her."

Suddenly, Billy turned and saw us. "Get over here!" he yelled. "You think I got nothing to do but wait for you?"

He threw our bikes in the truck's bed and told us to get in the cab. The back seat was barely big enough for Arthur and me, but it was better than riding out in the open with the bikes.

Before Billy started the engine, the rain hit the windshield in huge drops. To the east, a jagged fork of lightning shot across the sky, followed by a clap of thunder loud enough to make Nina and me jump.

Rocked by the wind, the truck lurched out of the weedy parking lot and onto the road. Every time we hit a bump, Arthur's and my knees and elbows jostled each other. His skinny little bones felt as sharp as iron rods.

Arthur leaned over the seat and said, "Don't you love thunderstorms, Nina? Can't you just see Thor up there, tossing his lightning bolts at the earth?"

She cringed at the sound of thunder, but Billy shook his head. "Thor," he snorted. "What are you talking about?"

"He's one of the most powerful Gods of the Aesir," Arthur said scornfully. "I thought *everybody* knew that."

Billy stopped the pickup so suddenly, we all flew forward. Turning to Arthur, he said, "If there's one thing I hate, it's a smart-mouth kid. You want to get out and walk home?"

"Sorry," Arthur muttered. I was glad he had enough sense to apologize. The rain was coming down so hard we might as well have been going through a car wash. "But—"

"Not everybody keeps their nose in a book, bud."

With that, Billy stepped on the gas. The tires slid on the gravel, and the pickup fishtailed a little. Nina cried out. I fastened my seat belt, but Arthur just gazed at the rain blurring the world outside his window. By some miracle, he seemed to have lost his appetite for talking.

"Please drive carefully, Billy," Nina said. "I hate thunder and lightning and rain."

"Say a prayer to Thor," Billy suggested.

No one laughed except Billy. Hunched over the steering wheel, he concentrated on driving. Though the upper part of his face was visible in the rearview mirror, I still couldn't see his eyes. He'd kept those sunglasses on, despite the steamy windshield and dark sky.

After that, nobody said anything. When we passed the Toot 'n' Tote, I said, "To get to our houses, turn right on the next street. Then—"

"You don't need to give me no directions," Billy muttered. "Everybody knows where the murder house is."

I slumped beside Arthur. Great. I lived in the "murder house." Everybody knew where it was. And what had happened in it.

At last Billy pulled into our driveway, and we hopped out to get the bikes.

Without looking at either Arthur or me, Billy slammed the pickup into reverse and backed out of the driveway. Nina leaned out her window and waved to us. "Bye, boys. Nice to see you again!"

Arthur and I stood under a big tree and watched the pickup splash off through sheets of water running across the road.

"What a creep." Arthur turned and started for home just as his grandmother stepped out on the porch, police whistle raised.

"Where have you been?" she hollered at him. "I was about to file a missing-persons report!"

"Riding bikes with Logan, and then the rain started." Arthur glanced at me and waggled his eyebrows as if he were warning me to keep my mouth shut about the Magic Forest.

That was fine with me. My parents would have grounded me for a week if they knew where I'd been.

"And guess who brought us home?" Arthur added. "Nina Stevens and Billy Jarmon."

"Nina was with Billy Jarmon?" Up went Mrs. Jenkins penciled eyebrows. "I told her to hire Johnny."

"Johnny was busy," Arthur said. "He told her to ask Billy."

Mrs. Jenkins sighed. "Well, I'm sure he can show her some interesting places."

With that, she herded Arthur across the yard and into the house. At the same moment the Jenkins's screen door slammed behind him, Mom appeared at our kitchen window and called me.

The minute I walked through the door, I got a long lecture on the importance of telling people where I was going and when I was coming back. I hemmed and hawed and fudged to keep from revealing where I'd actually been. But I said I was sorry and I apologized and agreed to all charges against me: yes, I was inconsiderate; yes, I was irresponsible; yes, I never thought of anyone but myself, and yes and yes and yes—guilty as charged.

When both Mom and Dad were finally convinced I was truly repentant, I was allowed to sit down at the kitchen table and have my dinner all by myself. My parents had already eaten. An hour ago, Mom pointed out with some vexation.

While I was dining on cold mashed potatoes, cold broccoli, and cold chicken, Dad sat down across from me. "Johnny said he saw you at the Toot 'n' Tote store on Route 23. What were you doing all the way out there?"

"Oh, Arthur was showing me more sights."

"Since when is a convenience store a sight?"

"In Bealesville, a traffic light is a sight," I said. "A dog peeing on a fire hydrant is a sight. A turtle crossing the road is a sight, a man trimming his hedge is a sight—"

"Okay, okay," Dad interrupted just as I was getting warmed up. "Johnny told me you were probably heading for the Magic Forest. He couldn't think of anything else in that direction."

"It's none of Johnny's business where Arthur and I go. What's it matter to him anyway?"

"According to Johnny, the park's full of falling-down ruins and is overrun with snakes," Dad went on as if he hadn't heard me. "It's also private property. If the police catch you in there, you'll be fined for trespassing."

"Arthur's gone there lots of times," I told him, "and he's never—"

"Just because his grandmother lets him wander all over the state of Virginia," Dad said, "doesn't mean you can do the same. Do you hear me?"

"Yes, I hear you." Picking up my empty plate, I carried it to the sink. "I'm kind of tired. Do you mind if I take a shower and go to bed?"

"It's only seven o'clock," Dad said.

"It was a long bike ride."

After my shower, I settled down in bed with my library book, but my brain was flashing with images of the Magic Forest and Billy and Nina. I wondered where they'd gone after Billy dropped Arthur and me in front of our houses. What if he asked her for a date? Would she go?

It was too disgusting to think about. If only I was older— if only, if only.

An hour or two later, Mom and Dad came upstairs, their voices loud in the quiet house. I put down my book and listened.

"Rhoda told me I should encourage Logan to join a team before school starts," Mom was saying. "She also said I should discourage him from making friends with a kid like Arthur."

"Rhoda, Rhoda, Rhoda," Dad muttered. "I'm so sick of hearing about Rhoda and her opinions on everything. If she thinks Arthur's unsuitable, I say encourage Logan to play with him."

"You and your weird sense of humor," Mom snapped. "Can't you ever take anything seriously?"

"I'm perfectly serious," Dad said. "Logan is old enough to

choose his own friends. And Rhoda has no business sticking her nose into our son's life."

"But Arthur is—"

"Arthur takes some getting used to," Dad said, "but he's a good kid. Smart, too. He even likes to read."

"He took Logan to that awful place—"

"I've talked to Logan about that. He realizes the danger. I don't think he'll go back there, but, even if he does—"

At that point, their bedroom door closed, and I heard no more.

"But even if he does, even if he does . . ." I lay back and grinned. Who knows what Arthur and I might do? I didn't have a clue myself. But whatever it was, it would be better than Little League. And it wouldn't be any of Rhoda's business.

9

The next morning, Arthur showed up again at breakfast time. Bear followed him in and wandered around the kitchen, sniffing at the door to the basement. I was glad Mom was in the living room arguing with Dad about what color to paint the house. If she'd seen the dog, she would have concluded he smelled Mrs. Donaldson's blood.

Without waiting for me to finish my cereal, Arthur plopped himself down in a chair and leaned toward me. "I've been thinking about that money," he said. "Didn't your dad say there's a ton of stuff in the attic that belonged to Mrs. Donaldson?"

I nodded. "Johnny's supposed to haul it to the dump today or tomorrow."

Arthur crammed some cereal into his mouth and chewed thoughtfully. "Maybe we should have a look at the attic before it's too late."

I knew Mom and Dad wouldn't want Arthur and me rummaging around in the attic, but they were still in the living room, too busy arguing to notice what we were up to.

With Bear behind us, we tiptoed up the steep, narrow steps. It must have been 150 degrees in the attic. The air was thick and heavy and smelled of dust and old things—paper and cardboard, wood and cloth. Dim light shone through the cobweb-covered windows at either end.

In the middle of the floor, I saw at least a dozen big, bulging cardboard cartons. It was obvious that someone had gone through every one of them. Worn-out shoes and clothes had been flung everywhere, along with books and records, dented pots and pans, photo albums, old bank statements, ragged towels, and torn sheets. A broken lamp lay on its side in the shadows under the eaves, along with an armchair, its upholstery clawed to shreds by cats. A china closet with cracked glass doors stood in a corner. One rusty roller skate sat on a stack of yellowing newspapers and magazines.

"Get a load of these." Arthur laughed and held up a huge pair of plaid boxer shorts. "Mr. Donaldson must've been as big as an elephant."

I laughed, too. But then I felt sad because the man had died a long time ago and never dreamed his wife would be murdered in their house and two kids would make jokes about his underwear.

Uneasy about looking at dead people's things, I sat back on my heels and wiped the sweat off my forehead. "The money's not here."

Arthur didn't answer. He was watching Bear nose through a box of old kitchen stuff, whimpering and whining to himself. "What are you after?" he asked the dog.

For an answer, Bear trotted over to Arthur and dropped a

small plastic bag at his feet. Wagging his tail, he barked once.

Arthur dumped the bag's contents on the floor. Out tumbled a handful of junky plastic toys, each about two inches tall. Some were red, some blue, some yellow, but they were all the same—eleven gingerbread men with smiling faces.

"They're from the Magic Forest gift shop," Arthur said. "I used to have lots of them—Snow White, the Crooked Man, Humpty-Dumpty, the Dish and the Spoon, even the Witch—but I sold them at one of Grandma's tag sales. All I got was a lousy quarter for the whole bunch."

He arranged the little gingerbread men in a row. "I should have kept mine," he said sadly. "By the time I'm grown up, they'll be worth a fortune on eBay."

I picked up a crumpled piece of pink note paper. "This must have fallen out of the bag."

Arthur snatched it from my hand. Squinting to make out the handwriting, he read,

"Dear Violet,

"When that money was embezzled from the Magic Forest, I had an idea who took it, but I never said anything to the police because I didn't have a shred of proof.

"I'm afraid to write his name, but while he was at lunch today, I searched his office. They're shutting the park down in a few days, and I knew he'd clean out his belongings. It was my last chance to prove he took the money, not me.

"I searched the file cabinet, the desk drawers, and, last of all, the coat closet. And there it was, stuffed way back on a high shelf where nobody would notice it—a briefcase with his initials on it. I'd seen it before. But not for a while.

"It was full of money, more money than I've ever seen, more than I ever imagined could be in one place. Like something you'd see in a movie but not in real life.

"There was no place to hide the briefcase in the ticket booth, and I was scared someone would see me carrying it out of the park. Since nobody was around just then, I hid it where we used to play the finding game with the little plastic gingerbread men. I hope you remember.

"It's safe there for now. I plan to go back and get it when no one's around to see me. If he notices it's gone before I go to the police, he might suspect I took it, so if anything happens to me, get the briefcase. Whatever you do, don't tell Silas until you've given it to the police.

"And don't be scared of You Know Who —she's just

Arthur stopped reading and peered at me, his eyes huge over the rims of his glasses.

"Go on," I said impatiently.

"That's all." He handed me the piece of paper. "It's dated the very day Mrs. Donaldson was murdered."

I read the note closely in case Arthur had left anything out. He hadn't. "Do you think the killer came while she was writing this?"

"He must have," Arthur's voice dropped to a whisper. "That's why she didn't finish it. Or even sign it."

He picked up one of the gingerbread men and studied its smiling plastic face. "The embezzler murdered her," he said in a low voice, "and then he ransacked the house, but he didn't find this bag."

"Even if he saw it, he wouldn't have thought it was important," I said. "Just a little plastic bag from the Magic Forest."

Arthur reread the note. "If we find the briefcase," he said slowly, "we'll know who killed Mrs. Donaldson."

We stared at each other. The attic was so quiet, I could hear a fly buzzing against one of the small windows. It was almost as if Mrs. Donaldson was watching us from the shadows, hoping we'd bring her murderer to justice and clear her name once and for all.

"What do you think she meant by the 'finding game'?" I asked.

Arthur shook his head. "I have no idea."

"And why did she write, 'Don't be scared of You Know Who'?"

He shook his head again. For once, he didn't have an answer.

While I reread the note, searching for hidden meanings, Arthur moved the gingerbread men into various formations, as if he hoped to break a code somehow. If he lined them up just right, the answers to our questions would be revealed.

"These little guys must have *something* to do with it," he mused. "But what?"

"Shh," I whispered. "Someone's coming upstairs."

Arthur scooped up the little men, dropped them into the bag along with the note, and stuffed everything into the deep pocket of his cargo shorts.

At the same moment, Bear ran to the top of the attic steps and began to bark. Arthur grabbed the dog's collar and pulled him away.

As Dad stepped into the attic, Bear stopped barking, but he kept up a low growl.

Johnny followed Dad. And behind him, I was shocked to see Billy, looking as surly as ever.

"What are you boys doing up here?" Dad asked. "It's hot enough to roast a turkey in this attic."

Billy looked as if he also wanted to know what we were doing. Without his sunglasses, his eyes were small and squinty and set too close together. He looked both stupid and mean, a bad combination.

I nodded my head toward Billy. "How come *he's* here?" I asked Dad. "You said Johnny was hauling the stuff away."

I glanced at Billy while I spoke. He was staring at me as if I were a bug he wanted to step on.

Dad gave me a puzzled look. "I can't imagine why you want to know," he said, "but Billy has a truck, and Johnny doesn't." Brushing the sweat out of his eyes, he added, "Unless you want to help us get rid of this stuff, go outside and find something else to do."

For a second I considered telling Dad exactly what kind of guys he'd hired, but I decided against it. Maybe I'd tell him later. When Billy or Johnny wasn't standing there, looking big and strong and tough.

With Bear at our heels, Arthur and I dashed down the steps, raced through the house, and sped out the back door.

"Get your bike," Arthur said. "We're going to the library and after that—we'll look for Violet at Wal-Mart."

W e made a quick stop at the library to make a photocopy of the note.

Arthur folded it and dropped it into his pocket. "It's always good to have a backup," he said. "Especially when the original is all you've got."

Wal-Mart wasn't as far as the Magic Forest, but there were plenty of big hills to climb between home and the store. As usual, Arthur was way ahead, standing up to pump, his skinny legs bulging with muscles the size of tennis balls. No matter what gear I used—and believe me, I tried them all— I couldn't keep up with him. Maybe he was training for that big French bike race.

When we finally pulled up at Wal-Mart's sliding doors, I chained my bike to a rack, and Arthur dumped his classic Raleigh on the sidewalk. Inside, the cold air smelled of popcorn, hot dogs, and unidentifiable synthetic substances. A cheap smell, Mom called it. But no matter how the store smelled, it was better than the heat outside.

We cruised up and down aisles, looking for Violet and

checking out the CDs, DVDs, and videos. In the electronics department, Arthur lingered over a stereo system with flashing LEDs, small enough to fit in a bookcase but loud enough to entertain the whole neighborhood. He fiddled with the bass and the treble, turned the volume up and down, and investigated the five-CD tray until I lost patience and dragged him away.

"We're looking for Violet," I reminded him.

Arthur scanned the store and pointed. "There she is—in office supplies. She's the one talking to a customer."

He started toward a clerk wearing the standard blue Wal-Mart vest over a yellow T-shirt and a pair of jeans. She didn't anywhere near resemble my image of the sort of person who'd marry someone like Silas. Too pretty, for one thing. And too fragile—she was so little and skinny, a gust of wind could probably strand her in a treetop. Nor did she look mean enough or old enough to be Danny's mother. She must have been thirteen or something when he was born.

When Arthur was about fifteen feet from Violet, he stopped so suddenly, his running shoes squeaked on the vinyl floor. Without a word of explanation, he dropped to his knees behind a display of school binders and pulled me down beside him.

"That man." He pointed. "The one she's talking to? It's not a customer—it's Silas."

I crouched beside Arthur and stared at the man. He was tall and lean, but his biceps bulged like he'd spent his whole life pressing iron. He was a lot older than Violet. And a lot bigger.

With her arms folded across her chest, Violet seemed to shrink into herself. She looked at the floor, not at Silas, her body tense. I had a feeling she was praying for a customer to come along and rescue her.

"I thought Silas was in jail," I whispered.

"Me, too."

Even though we couldn't hear what Silas was saying, he sounded mad. He kept jabbing his finger at Violet. She blinked every time he did it and stepped back. He moved forward when she moved back. Soon he had her up against shelves stocked with felt-tipped pens, crayons, pencils, and ballpoints. Trapped. No place to retreat.

"They're my kids, too," he said in a voice loud enough to startle a little girl who had just wandered over. Her mother shot Silas a worried look and hurried down the next aisle. For all she—or anyone—knew, Silas was about to pull out a gun and start firing. He was definitely the type to show up on the evening news, holding a dozen cops at bay while threatening to kill the Wal-Mart shoppers he'd taken hostage.

Instead of heading for the door like sensible people, Arthur and I sneaked closer to hear what Silas was going on about.

Violet cowered against the pens and said something in a low vioce.

"I don't care what your lawyer thinks!" Silas suddenly yelled, throwing in a few cuss words to describe the man. "They're my kids. I'll see them if I want to."

With that, he turned around and headed for the door.

Making sure Violet wasn't looking, Arthur followed him, and I followed Arthur. We watched Silas cross the parking lot and straddle a motorcycle. He gunned the engine and left with a roar loud enough to shatter glass. In a few seconds, he had disappeared into the traffic on Route 23.

Now that it was safe, Arthur and I hurried back to office supplies. Violet was tidying up the pens. She looked as if she might have been crying.

"Hey, Violet." Arthur walked up to her, grinning as if he'd just noticed her. "I haven't seen you for ages."

She turned and looked at him, her face blank. "I beg your pardon?"

Keeping up the cheerful act, he smiled broadly. "Don't you remember me?"

She studied his face for a moment. "Oh, my goodness—Arthur Jenkins. Of course I remember you. How's your grandmother these days?"

"She's fine, same as ever."

"Well, tell her hello for me."

"I will." Arthur turned to me. "This is Logan Forbes. He lives in your mother's old house."

"I heard someone bought it." Violet looked at me curiously, but I'd turned my attention to a display of notebooks. I wanted to tell her I was sorry about her mother being murdered, but I couldn't think of a good way to say something like that.

"Logan's dad's doing a lot of work," Arthur said. "The house is starting to look pretty good."

"Is Bear still hanging around?" Violet asked.

"Grandma and I took him in," Arthur said, "but he's at Logan's house most of the time."

"Danny wanted to keep Bear," Violet said, "but Silas said no. He hated that dog."

"Speaking of Silas," Arthur said, soul of tact that he was, "I saw him leaving the store when we were coming in. When did he get out of jail?"

Violet busied herself with a display of ballpoints in snazzy colors. "Last week," she said, moving on to a row of spiral-bound notebooks. "He's on probation. I don't know what they were thinking of, letting him out. He'll just get himself in trouble again."

"How much is this?" A woman in a flowered blouse and tight pink pants came up to Violet, holding a purple plastic file box. "I don't know why you people can't put prices on things."

As Violet took the box from the woman, Arthur said, "Can I ask you something important?"

"*Really* important," I added, finally getting the nerve to say something.

Violet looked puzzled. "Like what?"

"Do I have to get a manager for a price check?" the woman butted in. Scowling at me, she added, "My time is very important."

"So is mine," Arthur said.

"I'm sorry, ma'am." Violet led the woman away, but she called back to us, "Wait there. I'll only be a minute."

True to her word, Violet came back fast. Returning the purple file box to the shelf, she said, "She thought it was way too expensive. And a piece of junk."

Arthur handed her the little Magic Forest bag. "We found this in the attic. There's a note inside from your mother."

Violet gasped. "From my mother?" She pulled out the plastic gingerbread men. "Oh, my gosh, I used to play with these when I was little." Her eyes filled with tears, and she brushed them away with one hand.

"The note," Arthur said. "Read the note."

Violet smoothed the creases out of the paper. "It's Mom's handwriting," she whispered. More tears ran down her face. This time she ignored them.

When she'd read the note, she looked at Arthur. "I *knew* my mother didn't steal that money!"

"But she knew who *did* steal it," Arthur pointed out.

"It couldn't have been the park's owner. Mr. Farrell was a nice old man," Violet said. "When I was little, he let me ride the rides free and he gave me candy—little peppermints."

"Who else worked there?"

"I don't remember anybody but Mr. Farrell." Violet frowned. "No, wait. There *was* somebody else—he was hired long after I got too old for the Magic Forest. Mom complained about him all the time, but I don't remember his name. I'm sorry."

"What was the finding game?" Arthur asked. "What does it have to do with the briefcase?"

"I don't know." Violet shook her head sadly. "I haven't thought about the Magic Forest for years. It makes me too sad. Mom's dead, the park's closed—it's like my whole childhood is gone."

It was time to call it quits, I thought. At least for now. Violet had had enough of us.

But when I looked at Arthur, I could see he still had questions. I don't think he'd even noticed Violet was close to crying.

"How about 'You Know Who'?" he persisted. "Were you scared of some woman who worked in the park, somebody who knew the embezzler?"

"I was afraid of lots of things when I was little." She paused. "I still am," she added in a low voice, more to herself than us.

"Think, Violet, think," Arthur begged. "It has to be a woman—the note says 'she's just.' Just what?"

Violet wiped her eyes with the back of her hand. "There was a mean old lady who worked at the frozen-custard stand," she said slowly. "I was afraid to ask for a cone when she was working. But I don't see what she'd have to do with anything."

Before Arthur could ask another question, a sharp-faced little man interrupted us. "Too much talking, Ms. Phelps." Shooting a nasty look at Arthur and me, he added, "You boys need to buy something—or leave."

"Yes, sir, Mr. Phillips," Violet said. "They wanted some advice about school supplies, and I—"

"No excuses. I saw you wasting time earlier talking to a man. If it happens again, I'll put a comment in your file."

We watched him stalk off toward electronics, his baggy pant legs flapping around his ankles.

Violet scowled at the man's back. "He thinks being a manager at Wal-Mart is a really big deal."

"Sorry," I said. "We didn't mean to get you in trouble."

"It's okay. He's always mad at somebody."

"We'd better go." Arthur held out his hand for the bag.

"Please let me keep it," Violet said. "My mother wrote the note to me. And the little men—I thought they were gone forever." She gazed at us with those big sad eyes of hers.

Arthur and I looked at each other. I was kind of reluctant to let our only evidence go, but how could we say no? After all, we *did* have a copy of the note.

"Don't let anybody see it," Arthur said.

Violet pressed the bag to her heart. "It's my secret," she said. "Mom's and mine."

"And try to figure out what your mom meant about the finding game," Arthur said, "and not being scared."

Violet nodded, her face solemn with worry. "I will."

Outside, Arthur and I got our bikes and pedaled across the parking lot. After Wal-Mart's super-duper air-conditioned comfort, it was like riding into a wall of fire. Ahead of us, the asphalt shimmered in the heat.

We stopped at the edge of the road and waited for a break in the traffic. "Where to now?" I asked.

"Want to see the Phelps place?" Arthur asked. "Its definitely not to be missed. You can see the Jarmons' house, too. Two for the price of one—a real treat."

Without another word, he sped away, leaving me no choice except to follow in his wake.

11

After a half hour of steady uphill climbing, made even more fun by cars and trucks racing past just inches from my handlebars, Arthur turned off the highway. Soon we were making our way up an even steeper hill on a narrow dirt road that wound along the edge of a sharp drop-off. Not the sort of place to encounter a large vehicle—nowhere to go but off the road and down the hill into a rock-strewn gully. Certain death.

Finally, Arthur rounded a curve and came to a stop, skidding on loose gravel and dirt. "The Phelpses' house is up the hill on the left. The mobile home where Violet lives is behind it."

He wiped his sweaty face with his arm. "The Jarmons live on the other side of the road. They've got a bunch of mean dogs who hate bikes."

While I tried to convince myself I wasn't scared of the Jarmons or their dogs, Arthur dumped his old Raleigh in a thicket of honeysuckle and wild grape vine.

Sure I was making a big mistake, I laid my bike beside his. Keeping a screen of underbrush between ourselves and the road, we sneaked toward the houses. I had a feeling those dogs could smell us ten miles away, even if something like the old Berlin Wall separated us from them.

"Voilà, la maison Phelps." Arthur pointed to an old farm-house weathered to gray. Its roof was patched with sheets of plywood, and a pile of cinderblocks propped up one corner of the front porch. A vine—no doubt kudzu—covered most of the porch roof and hung from the eaves. Except for the satellite dish attached to a tree, some people might have described the place as picturesque in a ramshackle, run-down way—but not if they'd known anything about the inhabitants.

Its chrome shining, Silas's motorcycle leaned against the porch. My stomach plummeted—he must be home. That was bad, very bad.

Behind the house was a beaten-up old mobile home. From somewhere inside, a radio blasted '70s hard rock music, but no one was in sight.

"Look over there." Arthur pointed across the road. *"La maison Jarmon."*

The Jarmons' house was smaller and made of stone, but it was just as neglected. Two small cement lions sat on the porch, gazing across the overgrown lawn. At least a dozen skinny cats slept on the sagging roof of a rusted-out Geo Prizm, but the dogs were nowhere to be seen.

Crudely lettered signs nailed to trees warned strangers away. BEWAR VISHUS ATTAK DOGS, one said. NO TRESPASTING, said another. And scariest of all: HALF GUN WILL SHOOT.

The hot summer sun beat down on my bike helmet. Sweat ran down my spine. My T-shirt stuck to my skin. I felt dizzy from the heat and the endless buzzing of cicadas. I wanted to go home before the dogs attacked or a Jarmon came to the door and shot us with his half gun.

But before I had a chance to say, "Let's go," I saw Silas step out of the mobile home. Danny was right behind him.

From our hiding place, we watched Silas straddle his motorcycle.

"Give me a ride, Dad," Danny begged. "You promised." His voice had a nasal edge, almost a whine, that I hadn't noticed when I met him at the Toot 'n' Tote.

"Some other time. Maybe tomorrow."

"You said that yesterday," Danny said, definitely whining. "And the day before."

His dad shrugged, strapped on his helmet, and roared down the driveway with the throttle wide open. Danny watched him leave, his face creased with disappointment.

When Silas was out of sight, but not of hearing, Danny stood in the driveway, his head down, his shoulders drooping, kicking stones. I could almost have felt sorry for him. Almost. Not quite.

A skinny little girl appeared in the mobile home's doorway. Maybe five, maybe six, she wore a faded T-shirt and baggy shorts, and her hair was the color and texture of dental floss. "Is Daddy gone?"

"What do you think?" Danny muttered a few cuss words and went into the mobile home with the girl. The screen door slammed behind them like a gunshot.

"That was May," Arthur whispered. "Danny's little sister. Poor kid."

Just as I was about to suggest leaving, Billy's pickup rumbled into sight. Johnny was with him. In the back were the boxes from the attic bulging with Mrs. Donaldson's stuff. Ducking behind a tree, we watched Billy pull into the driveway. He and Johnny got out and began unloading the boxes.

Dumping the contents on the ground, they started pawing through the clothing, books, and newspapers.

"You really think you're going to find any money?" Johnny asked.

"She had it hid all over the house. Ask anybody."

"That's just a rumor, Billy. I was in and out of there a lot, doing yard work and stuff. I kept my eyes peeled, I can tell you, but I never saw an extra dollar bill. She could barely afford to pay me for cutting the grass."

"Then why did somebody kill her?"

Johnny shrugged. "Money was probably what he was after, but I doubt he got any."

"Maybe she hid it in the Magic Forest." Billy kicked a thick book across the yard. "Did you ever think of that?"

Johnny grimaced and wiped his sweaty face with his T-shirt. "If she hid it in that jungle, nobody will ever find it."

"A couple of million bucks is worth looking for, ain't it?"

Johnny shrugged. "That's just a rumor. Nobody knows for sure how much was missing."

Danny chose that moment to cross the road. "What are you guys doing with that old stuff?"

"Nothing." Billy kicked a box over and scowled at the books and records and photo albums that tumbled out. "Just junk."

Signaling to Johnny, he headed for the pickup.

"Can I come with you?" Danny asked.

Neither Billy nor Johnny answered. Leaving Mrs. Donaldson's stuff in the yard, they got into the truck and drove away.

Left behind again, Danny cussed all the swear words I'd ever heard and a few I hadn't. Then he pulled a low-slung bike out of the weeds and rode off, still cussing. I pitied anyone smaller than him who looked at him the wrong way.

"Come on," I said. "Let's get out of here before someone else comes along."

Just as we reached the place we'd hidden our bikes, the dogs crawled out from under the Geo, three of them, long and lean and mean. Part wolf from the look of them. Maybe all wolf. Barking like hellhounds, they came after us fast.

Arthur and I threw ourselves on our bikes and started pedaling faster than I thought possible. The dogs were right behind us, so close I swear I felt their hot breath on my bare legs. Just as I thought they had us, we crested the hill and started down. Bumping over ruts and skidding on loose gravel, we stayed on our bikes as if we were glued to the seats.

From the bottom of the hill we could hear the dogs barking, but they seemed to have lost interest in chasing us. Maybe they'd just wanted to scare us away. Well, I can tell you, they succeeded. My heart was beating so hard, I was afraid it would burst.

"Those dogs were bigger than the Hound of the Baskervilles and twice as vicious." I frowned at Arthur. "I'm never coming near this place again."

He pushed his sweaty hair back from his forehead, leaving it standing straight up. "As James Bond once said, 'Never say never.'"

"Never, never, never," I retorted.

When we finally got home, my legs ached. In fact, I almost fell down when I got off my bike. I was that sore. But before I had a chance to go inside and take a nap in the bathtub, Mrs. Jenkins beckoned to us from her back door.

"Somebody's here to see you boys," she called.

Violet was sitting at the kitchen table, looking as weary as I felt. The plastic gingerbread men were scattered across the table.

Arthur grabbed a couple of cold cans of soda from the refrigerator and handed me one. "I don't know whether to drink it," he said, "or pour it over my head."

"I say drink it." I flopped down at the table, tipped the can back, and gulped it down so fast, I almost choked.

"Violet showed me the note from her mother," Mrs. Jenkins said. "We've been sitting here trying to figure out what game she meant."

Across the table from me, Violet toyed with a green gingerbread man. "Remember the map of the Magic Forest they used to give you when you bought a ticket?" she asked Arthur.

He nodded. "There were little pictures of all the attractions. Willie, the castle—"

"If I looked at one," Violet said, "maybe I'd remember the finding game."

"I bet the library has plenty of them in the local-history file," Arthur said. "Want me to get one for you?"

"I'd go myself," Violet said, "but I work the nine-to-six shift tomorrow, the same hours the library's open." She pushed her chair back and gathered up her things. "I have to go home and fix dinner for the kids."

At the door, Mrs. Jenkins gave her a hug. "You be careful, honey. Being divorced isn't enough to keep Silas away. Any trouble, you call me. Come over if you like. Bring the kids. We've got an extra bedroom."

Arthur raised his eyebrows in mock horror and ran a finger across his throat. Neither one of us wanted Danny Phelps staying at Arthur's house.

The next morning, Arthur and I rode our bikes to the library. He headed straight to a row of gray filing cabinets against the rear wall. Dropping to his knees, he opened a bottom drawer labeled LOCAL HISTORY, L–N. Flipping through the folders, he pulled one out and waved it at me.

"*Voilà!*" he cried. "The Magic Forest!"

We sprawled on the floor and started going through the folder. Stuck in with old photographs and newspaper clippings was a map of the Magic Forest, showing a wide path looping around Willie the Whale's Pond. Smaller paths branched off, leading to kiddie rides and other attractions: the Old Woman's Shoe, Peter Pumpkin's Shell, Cinderella's Coach, Mother Hubbard's Cupboard, the Witch's Hut.

"Uh-oh," I said, "It's stamped 'reference only.'"

"So?"

"So that means you can't check it out."

"Who said anything about checking it out? We can make a photocopy."

"Do you have any money?"

"No, but you must have some."

I turned my pockets out to show they were empty.

Arthur swore a little swear. Then, taking a quick look around, he stuffed the map into his pocket.

"Arthur—"

"Shh. We need this more than anybody else I can think of." With that, he headed for the door, pausing on his way out to wave to Mrs. Bailey in the children's room. "We'll bring it back," he whispered to me, "after Violet figures out where her mother hid the briefcase."

First trespassing. Now stealing. No, not stealing—informally borrowing. What would Arthur think of next?

Although I was positive an alarm would go off, no one stopped us from sauntering out into the steaming July heat.

"Where to now?" I asked wearily.

"Wal-Mart," he said. "Where else?"

Grabbing our bikes, we sped away, unnoticed, uncaught, criminals in the making. We might as well have been part of the Jarmon/Phelps extended family.

12

At Wal-Mart, we found Violet at her usual station in office supplies, trying to look busy tidying the displays.

"We brought you a map of the Magic Forest." Arthur held out the wrinkled sheet of paper.

"You'd better keep it for now." Violet's eyes filled with tears. "Silas took the note," she whispered.

I stared at her, too shocked to speak, but Arthur made up for my silence. "What do you mean 'Silas took the note'? How did he get it?"

Violet straightened a row of notebooks. "He came over last night." Her face colored. "I wasn't expecting him. He barged right in demanding to see Danny, and he saw me reading the note. He snatched it out of my hand like he thought— Well, I don't know what he thought. But when he saw it was from Mom, he took it."

"Where is he now?" Arthur looked around as if he expected to see Silas lurking behind a rack of school supplies.

"He said something about going to the library," Violet said, "which struck me as really weird because I've never seen him pick up a book, let alone read one. No," she corrected herself, "he used a dictionary once to prop open a window."

Arthur looked at me. "That reminds me. Grandma wanted me to see if the new Mary Higgins Clark mystery has come in. She's got it on reserve."

"But we were just there. Why—"

Arthur shook his head. "Come on, Logan."

"I don't want to see Silas—"

Arthur towed me toward the door. "Let's go."

"Wait a minute," Violet called after us. "Tell your grandmother I'll be coming over tonight with Danny and May. Not for long. Just a couple of nights."

"Yeah, sure, that's a great idea," Arthur said, trying to sound sincere. "Maybe Silas will steal a car or do a little breaking and entering or shoot somebody and get sent back to jail. Then you won't have to worry about him."

Violet tried to smile again—a little more successfully this time. "We can always hope."

As soon as we were outside Wal-Mart's big sliding glass doors, I said to Arthur, "Tell me why we're going to the library twice in one day. We've got the map. What else do we—"

Arthur cuffed my arm lightly. "Think, Logan, think! Why is Silas going to the library?"

Feeling stupid, I stared at Arthur. "To get . . . a map?"

Arthur nodded. "There were at least two more in the folder. We should've taken them all to keep him from getting one."

• • •

By the time we got to the library, our clothes were soaked through with sweat, and I was beginning to hate my bike helmet. It made my head feel as if I'd stuck it in an oven.

Mrs. Bailey looked up and smiled when we passed her desk. "Back again so soon? Did you forget something?"

Arthur nodded and kept going, with me practically stepping on his heels. We squatted down by the file cabinet, yanked open the bottom drawer, and took out the Magic Forest folder.

"Here's another map," I said, rooting one out.

Arthur grabbed a third one out of the folder and deftly slipped both of them into the deep pockets of his cargo shorts.

As I grabbed another one, I heard a familiar voice. "I'm looking for stuff about the Magic Forest. You got any old maps or anything like that?"

From the floor, I peeked around a bookcase. Silas stood at the adult-services desk. Mrs. Jones, the reference librarian, was getting up to show him the filing cabinets.

On all fours, Arthur and I crawled to the men's room as fast as we could go. Crowding into the only stall, we locked the door. My heart pounded, and Arthur's face was dead white. His fingers trembled when he shot the bolt into place.

"Did he see us?" he asked.

"I don't think so, but a lot of other people did." I remembered two or three adults scowling at us. One woman had muttered something about kids horsing around in the library. Apparently, I'd crawled right over her foot in my haste to reach the men's room.

We waited in the stall for a few long minutes. After a while,

Arthur said, "Look out the door and see if he's still there." When I hesitated, he gave me a little shove. "Go on, Logan. It's boring in here."

I left him in the stall and opened the men's room door—just wide enough to look out. The file cabinets were in plain view. Mrs. Jones was going through the contents of the folder we'd left on the floor.

"That's funny," she said. "There should be several maps in here."

"Did somebody check them out?" Silas asked.

"No, they're clearly stamped 'reference only,'" she said.

"I saw some boys looking at that folder," a woman said, the very one whose foot I'd crawled across. "They were making a mess of everything in it."

"Do you know where they went?" Silas asked.

She pointed at the men's room. "They're probably wrecking the plumbing in there or writing dirty words on the walls."

Like a dog who's just caught the scent of something interesting, Silas looked toward the men's room. I shut the door and ran back into the stall, bolting it with fumbly fingers.

"He knows we're in here."

As I spoke, the men's room door opened. Arthur and I cowered in the stall, sure we were about to be drowned in the toilet or something equally horrible.

Instead of Silas, Mrs. Jones said, "Arthur, you come out of there right now!"

Without consulting me, Arthur opened the stall door. "We

weren't doing anything," he said in his most innocent voice. "Honest."

"Come here, Arthur." Mrs. Jones looked at me. "You, too."

I followed Arthur out of the men's room. Silas watched us go to Mrs. Jones's side. His face was unreadable, but his eyes scared me. If looks could kill, we'd be on our way to the funeral home.

"That's the boy." The irate woman pointed at me. "He was crawling on the floor. He went right over my foot. I have bunions, you know. It was very painful."

"I'm sorry," I said. "I didn't know you had bunions." I meant every word. Even though she hadn't planned to, the crabby old lady had probably saved Arthur's and my lives.

Unfortunately, Arthur giggled. "Bunions" is a funny word when you think about it, but at that moment nothing could have made me laugh—not with Silas staring at me with those eyes of his.

"And what do you find so amusing?" the woman asked Arthur.

"Um . . . nothing," he muttered, choking back laughter.

Mrs. Jones took us each by an arm. "Marie, I'm so sorry these boys were rude to you," she said. "It must be the heat. They're usually nice, well-mannered kids."

"If I were you, I'd suspend their library privileges." Mrs. Bunions started to walk away but turned back to add, "I'd also have your maintenance man check the men's room. There's no telling what they might have done in there."

"Come along, boys," Mrs. Jones said. "I have some chores for you in the work room." Taking us through the STAFF ONLY door, she sat us down at a long table and handed us each a stack of blank cards and a rubber stamp.

"I don't know what's gotten into you, Arthur. Crawling on the floor like a child. Annoying people." Mrs. Jones glanced at me as if I were somehow to blame for Arthur's unusual behavior. "But I might as well get some use out of you and your new friend. Stamp due dates on these cards, and all will be forgiven." She winked at Arthur as she spoke. "Just between us, Marie Pertle is a pain in the neck—but her husband's on the library board."

With that, Mrs. Jones returned to the reference desk. Before she closed the door, I saw Silas slumped in a chair, facing us. Although he had a magazine in his lap, he wasn't reading. He was waiting for us to come out.

"What do we do now?" I asked Arthur.

Arthur raised his head. He'd already managed to smear ink all over his fingers and chin. He'd also stamped "9/3/09" on his arm like a tattoo. "That's the date school starts," he said. "It's a good way to remember, don't you think?"

"If we're still alive by then." I grabbed the stamp before he could put a date on my arm. "How can you goof around at a time like this? Didn't you see Silas sitting in that chair by the door? He'll wait there all day for us."

Arthur shrugged. "Let him."

"Are you nuts?" I could feel the adrenaline racing through my veins, preparing me for danger, flight, self-defense, whatever it took to stay alive. "The library closes at six. What happens then?"

Ignoring me, Arthur got to his feet and walked calmly toward the back of the workroom. He might have been on his way to church or out for an evening stroll.

"Where are you going?"

He didn't answer, so I followed him. He was standing by a pair of double metal doors, painted industrial gray. "This is the delivery entrance," he said. "Coming?"

Looking both ways, we darted across the loading dock. Behind us the door swung shut. And locked with a click.

We were at the end of an alley. Around the corner, I could see our bikes in the library rack.

With my adrenaline at an all-time high, I ran after Arthur, wrested my bike free, and flung myself into the saddle. Pedaling with all our might, we zoomed past the Rite Aid drugstore just as Nina stepped off the curb. Trying to avoid her, I lost control of my bike and plowed into Arthur. We both hit the road with a clash of metal.

Nina stared down at us, clutching a plastic bag from the drugstore. "Are you all right?"

The two of us scrambled to our feet, desperately trying to untangle ourselves from our bikes.

"Your knee's bleeding." Nina took my arm. "Come into the drugstore. The pharmacist will wash that out and bandage it."

"No." I pulled away. "It's just a scrape. My mom will take care of it."

"But, Logan—" she began.

"We have to go!" Despite my injury, I jumped on my bike and sped away, just behind Arthur. I hated to be rude to Nina, but not far off I could hear a motorcycle revving up.

"It's Silas!" Arthur yelled.

Dead ahead was the cemetery, its fancy iron gates open and welcoming. Arthur pedaled straight toward them as fast as he could go, and I raced after him.

13

Half blinded by sweat dripping in my eyes, I followed Arthur through the gate and down a shady side road. Suddenly, he veered across a patch of grass and vanished into a grove of trees. I was right behind him. Dragging our bikes with us, we crawled under a willow's long, drooping branches. From our hiding place in the dark green shade, we watched for Silas. A woman walked by pushing a stroller. Three joggers passed her. A kid walking a dog stopped to talk to the woman.

"I don't think he's coming," I whispered.

"It could be a trick," Arthur said. "We'd better sit tight for a while, just in case he's waiting for us to come out."

The ground was bare and damp under the trees. Their roots spread out, humping above the earth into a network of comfortable sitting places. Mourning doves sobbed and cicadas thrummed, getting louder and softer, louder and softer as if nothing else mattered.

"How did you ever find this place?" I asked.

"Danny and his gang chased me into the cemetery once.

This is where I hid," he said. "I come here a lot now. It's a good place to read and think about stuff."

"But it's a cemetery," I reminded him. "Doesn't that bother you?"

"I'm more scared of living people than dead people," Arthur said.

Considering our present circumstances, he definitely had a point. Cautiously, I parted the willow's long branches and peered out. "I don't see Silas."

"We'd better stay here a while longer, just in case."

"Yeah." I turned my attention to my knee. It had stopped bleeding, but it was pretty dirty. I hoped I was right about it just being a little scrape. Otherwise, it could get infected and I could get septicemia and die. At least that would save Silas the trouble of killing me.

Arthur reached into his shorts' pocket, pulled out one of the library's maps, and spread it on the ground between us. Along the Magic Forest's winding paths, an illustrator had drawn and labeled all the park's attractions—rides, buildings, nursery rhyme figures, statues.

He pointed at the picture of Old Mother Hubbard's Cupboard. "That was the refreshment stand. They had the best frozen custard in the whole world. Boy, would I love to have some right now."

I studied the map, trying not to think how a double dip of frozen custard would cool my mouth and slide down my throat and fill my lunchless stomach. "It's weird thinking all that stuff is hidden under kudzu now. The paths, the buildings, the statues. Even with a map, I don't see how we'll find anything."

"Not everything's covered up. You saw those statues sticking out of the kudzu—Alice in Wonderland, the Dish running away with the Spoon, Humpty-Dumpty. And Willie the Big Blue Whale." Arthur ran his finger along a path on the map. "Look—there's a fence made of gingerbread men leading to the Witch's Hut. I'd forgotten all about that."

"They look just like the little plastic men."

Arthur turned to me. "Do you think Mrs. Donaldson was trying to tell Violet that the briefcase is hidden near the hut?"

"Maybe." I studied the drawing of the little hut. "Is it still there?"

"I haven't been to that part of the park since it closed," Arthur said. "There's no way to know what's there unless we go and look."

Unless we go and look. He made it sound as if the Magic Forest was our fate, our destiny. Go there and find the money—or die trying.

Arthur continued to study the map as if he intended to stay in the cemetery for hours, but I was getting restless. The root was starting to feel hard under my butt. I was hungry. And thirsty. And hot. I didn't want to think about the Magic Forest or the evidence or the murder anymore. "Can we go home now?"

Arthur parted the willow's branches, and we gazed out at the cemetery. The late-afternoon sunlight cast long shadows across the grass. An old couple ambled past, walking a dog as ancient as they were. Otherwise, the place seemed to be deserted.

We dragged our bikes from our hiding place, but before

we rode away, Arthur paused to point out a statue of a woman and her little boy. The woman had an open book in her lap, and the boy stood beside her, looking up into her calm marble face.

"That's Eleanor Beale and her son, Arthur," he told me. "Arthur, just like me."

He touched Arthur Beale's marble shoe reverently. "Eleanor was married to Robert Bradley Beale, the guy the town was named for. There's a statue of him in the park downtown."

I sat on the seat of my bike, one foot on the pedal, ready to go, but Arthur went on talking in a quiet voice. "I used to pretend Eleanor Beale was my mother, and I was her little boy, and we were reading that book together. Sometimes if no one was around, I'd even climb into her lap. Dumb, huh?"

"What happened to your real mother?" I asked. "You never talk about her."

Arthur leaned on his bike's handlebars, his eyes on the statue's face. "There's nothing to say. I've been living with Grandma since I was a baby."

"Is your mother dead?" I asked softly.

He shrugged. "What difference does it make whether she's dead or alive? I never see her. She never calls, she never writes. Not to me or Grandma. She's probably a drug addict. Or worse."

I'd never heard anyone say such things about his mother. "You don't care about her at all?"

Arthur gripped his handlebars so tightly his knuckles whitened. "She doesn't care about me. Why should I care about her?" He glanced at me, and I saw the glint of tears behind his glasses.

Sad and embarrassed, I looked down at the gravel path. A line of black ants paraded by as if they were engaged in important business. "How about your dad?"

"My mother showed up one day at Grandma's house," Arthur went on, as if he hadn't heard me. "She had me with her. The infant. No explanations. A couple of weeks later she left." Arthur bent his head over his handlebars and fiddled with his bike gears. "Without me. And that was that."

I tried to think of something to say, but nothing came to mind except stupid remarks like "That's awful." I patted his back silently, hoping he'd understand how bad I felt for him.

"It's okay," he muttered. "Like I said, I don't care anymore." Without another word, he began pedaling away, leaving Mrs. Beale and her son to gaze forever at the same page in their stone book.

Just to be safe, we rode home the back way, zipping down alleys and cutting across back yards. To our relief, we didn't meet Silas or anyone else.

Mom was sitting on the porch, reading a mystery novel as usual. When she saw me, she frowned. "It's about time you got here, Logan. You missed lunch, and now it's almost time for dinner."

Arthur poked his elbow in my side and gestured toward his yard. Violet's old car was parked out front. May sat on the grass, making a clover chain, and Danny was tossing a ball for Bear to catch. He looked happier than usual.

From the porch steps, Mrs. Jenkins called, "Come on over here, Arthur. Bring Logan with you."

I glanced at Mom, sure she'd order me inside, but she was lost in her book again.

Reluctantly, Arthur and I headed toward his house.

Danny stopped tossing the ball and stared at us. "Just because I'm staying here doesn't mean I'm your friend or nothing." He kept his voice low, too low for Mrs. Jenkins to hear.

"I assure you the feeling is mutual," Arthur said, affecting an English accent for reasons known only to him.

Danny scowled. "You're weird. You know that? Nuts. Crazy."

Arthur shoved his glasses back up to the bridge of his nose. "At least I'm not stupid."

By now Mrs. Jenkins was crossing the lawn, a big smile on her face. "Logan, have you met Danny?"

Before I could answer, Arthur said, "Logan had the dubious pleasure of meeting Danny at the Toot 'n' Tote."

"They say two's company and three's a crowd, but I'm sure you boys will get along just fine." Mrs. Jenkins smiled again, clearly determined to see things in the most optimistic light. "Come inside and cool off with some soda."

May slipped her clover chain over her head and followed us to the kitchen. Violet was sitting at the table, her chin propped on her hand, her eyes sad and distant. The little girl pulled the clover chain off and gave it to Violet. "I made this for you, 'cause you're pretty and I love you."

"Thank you, May." Violet hugged her daughter. "That's

very sweet of you." For some reason, she looked as if she was about to cry.

Mrs. Jenkins patted her shoulder. "You're lucky to have such a sweet child."

Violet nodded, looking even more tearful.

Danny came inside with Bear. "When we go home," he told Arthur and me, "this dog's coming with us."

"Oh, no, he's not," Arthur said. "We've been taking care of him ever since your . . ." Catching a warning look from Mrs. Jenkins, Arthur left his sentence hanging.

"Bear's my dog." Danny turned to his mother. "Isn't he?"

Violet shook her head. "We can't afford a dog. You know that."

Danny slumped at the table, his legs stuck out, his face ugly. "I never get nothing I want," he muttered.

Violet reached out to pat his arm, but he jerked away from her.

In the silence, Mrs. Jenkins busied herself handing out sodas. Pointing to an open bag of cookies, she said, "Help yourselves."

The whole time we ate and drank, no one said anything except May. Climbing onto her mother's lap, she whispered, "Don't be sad, Mommy."

"I'm not sad." Violet blew her nose on the tissue Mrs. Jenkins handed her.

Nobody was fooled. Not even May, who sat there quietly and stroked Violet's arm, her face almost as unhappy as her mother's.

Violet turned to me suddenly and forced herself to smile.

"Mom's house looks much better now. More like it did when I was little." She sighed. "I hated seeing it so tumbledown."

"I'll tell Dad you like it," I said. "He's been doing a lot of work."

Violet blew her nose again, and I stole a glance at Danny. He sat there eating his cookies as if they were enemies, biting into them fiercely, chewing hard, and swallowing noisily. He didn't look at anyone. And he didn't say a word.

Finally, I heard Mom calling me to come home. Glad to escape, I excused myself and headed for the back door. Arthur followed me outside.

"There's only one extra room," he muttered. "Violet and May must be sleeping there. You know what that means?"

"You get a roommate?"

"It's not funny!" Arthur glared at me. "How would you like to sleep in the same bed as Danny Phelps?"

"Just be glad it's not Silas." With that, I took a flying leap from the porch and darted through the gap in the hedge. "See you tomorrow!" I shouted at Arthur, but he just looked at me, his face glum.

14

After dinner, I was watching an old *Sopranos* rerun when the phone rang. Thinking it might be Arthur, I ran to answer it. To my amazement, it was Nina. First of all, she asked if my knee was okay. I couldn't believe she'd called just to ask about a cut, but I told her it was fine. Mom had doused it with something that stung like mad and then slapped a big Band-Aid on it. "They won't have to amputate after all," I joked.

Nina laughed politely and asked if she could speak to Mom.

"Did you find out something new about the murder?" I asked.

"No," she said. "I just want to talk to her."

There was something odd about her voice. With some misgiving, I handed the phone to Mom and went back to the living room. On TV, a bunch of guys were shooting at each other from speeding cars. The noise of the show drowned out Mom's conversation with Nina.

After a while, Mom walked into the living room and turned off the TV.

"Hey, what are you doing?" I asked. "I'm watching that!"

"I want to talk to you," she said. "Right now."

She stood over me, her arms folded across her chest. I didn't like the look on her face. She knew something, I was sure of it—but I didn't know what. The situation made me very uncomfortable.

"Nina Stevens just told me you and Arthur got into trouble at the library today."

My heart dropped to the bottom of my belly. "She wasn't there. How could she possibly—"

"Someone told her all about it."

"Nina knows Mrs. Bunions?" I stared at Mom, amazed.

"It doesn't matter *who* told her," she said. "What matters is that you and Arthur slung file folders all over the library and scattered maps and pamphlets on the floor. Then you vandalized the men's room."

My amazement turned to disbelief. "*Nina* told you this?"

"And that's not all. You stole valuable material from the local-history file." Mom stared at me, her eyes filled with tears. "Oh, Logan, how could you behave like that? You were brought up properly. You come from a good home—"

"Wait, wait." I held my hands up. "All Arthur and I did—"

"Arthur, Arthur, Arthur!" Mom spoke so loudly, I was scared Arthur would think she was calling him and come running. "Do you know how sick I am of seeing that boy stuffing my food into his face? He has no manners, he comes and goes as if he lived here he—"

"But, Mom—"

"I don't want that boy in my yard or in my house."

I stared at her, bewildered by her anger. "What do you mean? He's my only—"

"Nina is also concerned about your friendship with him," Mom cut in. "She and I agree it would be best for you to—"

"Don't believe Nina. She's lying, she—"

"Arthur is off limits!" Mom talked right over me, as relentless as a steamroller flattening asphalt. "His grandmother pays no attention to where he goes or what he does. And he drags you along with him. He's a bad influence, a—a—"

She caught her breath, her face red with anger. "Let's just say Arthur is *not* the sort of boy I want my son to associate with. If you continue to hang out with him, you'll have no friends in middle school. Is that what you want? To be a misfit like Arthur?"

I stared at Mom in disbelief. "Please don't do this," I begged her. "Nina must be crazy, she—"

Dad poked his head into the living room. "What's Logan done now?" He spoke in a joking way, but Mom wasn't in the mood for his humor.

"Go to bed," she told me. "We'll talk about this in the morning."

Knowing it was useless to argue, I dragged myself upstairs. Instead of getting into bed, I sat on the windowsill and tried to get my mind around Nina's motives for telling Mom a pack of lies. I was sure she hadn't been in the library to witness Arthur's and my behavior. Nor did I think Mrs. Jones or Mrs. Bailey would concoct a story like that about Arthur and me.

So who, what, why?

And then it came to me—the only explanation. Silas had

told Nina about Arthur's and my behavior in the library. *Silas.* Nina knew Silas. She'd believed everything he'd told her.

Utterly miserable, I sat and stared at Arthur's dark house. I'd liked Nina, I'd trusted her, I'd admired her. And what had she done but betray Arthur and me with lies? I never wanted to see her again.

The next morning, I rushed downstairs in time to see Arthur standing at the kitchen door. Mom faced him, her back to me, her shoulders squared. If I'd dared to hope she was over being mad, I was wrong.

"I'm sorry," she was saying, "but Logan and I have something to do today."

"Like what?" Arthur pressed his face against the screen, but Mom didn't invite him in. "Maybe I could come, too," he said. "I don't have anything special planned."

"Not today."

"But—"

"You heard me," Mom said in her coldest voice.

Arthur turned away as if he knew the game was up. From the back, his shoulder blades poked against his faded T-shirt.

"Mom," I began, but she shut me up by grabbing my arm and hustling me out of the kitchen.

"What's the matter with you?" I yelled. "You were really rude to Arthur. He's my friend and—"

Mom gave me a little shake. "I told you last night you were not to associate with Arthur."

"But—"

She held out her hand. "Give me what you took from the

pamphlet file, Logan. Then we'll go to the library, and you can return it—with apologies."

Despite myself, I turned away. "I don't have it," I muttered.

Mom tilted my chin up so I had to face her. "Look me in the eye and say that, Logan."

"Arthur has it." I was telling the truth—or at least part of it.

Mom shifted her attention to my cargo shorts. "What's in your pocket?"

"Nothing." I backed away, but Mom grabbed my arm.

"Show me," she said.

Reluctantly, I produced the map. "It's just an old—"

She snatched it and saw the library stamp. "Oh, Logan," she said. "I'm so disappointed in you."

"You don't understand, Mom. If you make me take it back to the library, these really bad guys will get it. That's why we took it—to keep them from finding . . ."

Mom stared at me as if she'd never seen me before. "Is this some craziness Arthur dreamed up?"

"Why can't you trust me?" I was yelling now, but I didn't care. "Why take Nina's word over mine? I'm your son!"

"Stop shouting at me, Logan!"

Dad came to the kitchen door. He was holding a brush dripping with moss green paint. Johnny was right behind him, Dad's shadow.

"What's going on now?" Dad asked.

Mom waved the map at Dad. "Your son stole this from the library! He and Arthur!"

Dad looked at the map and then at me, obviously puzzled. "Why did you take some useless thing like this?"

Behind him, Johnny stared at me with interest, but I kept my mouth shut. I wasn't about to say anything important in front of him.

"Arthur's been a terrible influence on Logan," Mom told Dad, eager to blame my one and only friend for everything.

"Stop picking on Arthur!" I yelled.

"That's enough," Mom said. "Come along now."

As Mom rushed me outside and into the car, I heard Johnny say, "I told him to dump Arthur. Nobody likes that kid. He's weird. Crazy."

When we pulled away from the house, I saw Arthur sitting on his front steps, shoulders hunched, watching us glumly. I waved, and he lifted his hand in farewell.

Behind him, Danny sulked in the doorway, his nose pressed to the screen. Bear sat beside him.

Although I argued with Mom all the way to the library, she paid no attention to a word I said. She'd made her plans, set her goals, organized her priorities. Nothing would alter her decision.

Mrs. Bailey and Mrs. Jones were chatting at the information desk. When they saw me, they smiled and said hi—which they surely wouldn't have done if Arthur and I were guilty of the things Nina had accused us of doing.

"I'm Logan's mother, Carolyn Forbes," Mom said. "Logan has come to apologize for his behavior yesterday."

Before I could say a word, Mrs. Jones said, "Logan and Arthur were just horsing around, acting silly. I gave them some work to do. And then they went on their way."

"They didn't vandalize anything?" Mom asked.

"No, of course not."

"They're good kids," Mrs. Bailey put in. "It's been so nice to see Arthur with a friend."

Mom looked surprised to hear this, but she went on with her agenda anyway. "Logan has something to return to you."

Red-faced, I handed the Magic Forest map to Mrs. Jones. "I took this," I mumbled. "I'm sorry, but—"

Mrs. Jones looked at the map. "For heaven's sake, I've been searching all over for this. A man asked for one yesterday. We're supposed to have several, but I couldn't find any of them."

She paused and stared at me. "Why didn't you make a photocopy?"

"I didn't have any money," I said, "and we—"

The librarians glanced at each other. "Does Arthur by any chance have the other maps?" Mrs. Jones asked.

"I don't mean to be rude," I said, "but Arthur's my friend. I can't tell on him."

"He's not your friend anymore," Mom said. Turning to Mrs. Jones, she added, "I suggest you call Arthur's grandmother if you want the rest of the maps."

As she led me away, I asked her why she didn't just call the police. "Maybe they'd send me to jail and you wouldn't have to put up with me any longer."

"That's not a bad idea," she snapped in a sort of joking way.

On the way to the car, she stopped to look in the dry cleaner's window. "What are all these posters about saving the Magic Forest? I thought a big development was planned for the property."

"Arthur says a lot of people in town don't want a zillion newcomers moving in here."

Mom frowned at the sound of Arthur's name. "In Rhoda's opinion, the people opposed to it are fighting progress. What's wrong with a population increase? We'll have a larger tax base, better schools, decent places to shop and eat."

I felt like saying Rhoda was a worse influence on Mom than Arthur was on me, but what was the use—she'd just get mad.

"The bulldozing's scheduled to begin soon," Mom went on. "I don't think there's much hope of 'saving the magic.'"

We got back in the car. The seats were so hot from the sun, I expected to get second-degree burns on the back of my legs.

"Are we going home now?"

Mom shook her head. "I talked to Rhoda last night. She has a son your age, and we thought it would be fun to get you two together. School begins in a couple of weeks. Wouldn't it be nice to make a new friend?"

"I already have a friend," I muttered.

A grim look settled on Mom's face. Full of resolution, she headed the car out of town and into Fair Oaks, which meant passing between two curving stone walls. I expected an armed guard to stop us and demand to see our IDs.

Big houses with huge windows and multilevel decks sat in the middle of landscaped lots. The grass was a uniform green, the trees and flower beds were planted in symmetrical perfection, and NEIGHBORHOOD WATCH signs sprouted on every corner.

After negotiating a series of winding streets with names like Trembling Aspen, Summer Hat, and Woven Fancy, Mom finally stopped in front of a big stone-fronted house with hanging flower baskets swaying from the porch rafters.

Rhoda waved from the front door. "Come in, come in," she called. "Glad to see you, Logan. I've heard so much about you." She shook my hand firmly. Her hair was colored—even I could tell that—and she wore makeup and expensive clothes, and lots of jewelry, too. Though I hated to agree with anything Billy Jarmon said, she really did look slick enough to sell George's picture off a one-dollar bill.

She led us into air-conditioned perfection of the sort you encounter in model houses where no one lives. Everything smelled new. No mess, nothing out of place. In other words, the interior was even more boring than the exterior.

Mom looked around, taking in the ivory carpet and the dried-flower arrangements and the furniture. "Oh, Rhoda, it's beautiful. I love it."

Rhoda smiled modestly. "I'm sure your darling little house has much more charm. And think of its potential."

"It's a work in progress," Mom said. "It takes Hank forever to finish anything. He and Johnny are still painting the exterior. Heaven knows when they'll get around to the rest of the house."

"Tell me about it." Rhoda rolled her eyes, obviously agreeing that all men were undependable, unreliable, and slow.

"Well, now." Rhoda turned to me. "The boys are in the family room playing video games."

Reluctantly, I followed her down a flight of carpeted steps to a large room with sliding glass doors. Outside, a deck bloomed with potted plants and more hanging flower baskets.

"Here's Logan," Rhoda called to the three boys crowded around a large-screen computer where action heroes dashed through a labyrinth, lobbing fireballs at menacing hooded figures popping up here and there. The graphics were incredible, but the game itself seemed to be based on the same old formula of good guys and bad guys going at each other with loud sounds and spurts of blood and brains.

The boys got to their feet slowly and faced Rhoda and me. "Logan, this is my son, Anthony," she said. "Boys, meet Logan Forbes. From Richmond."

A tall boy with dark hair smiled politely. "Glad you could come over, Logan." He sounded as if his mother had told him what to say.

"These two young men live in the neighborhood," Rhoda went on. "Robert Oliver and Mackenzie Stone. They're practically part of the family."

Robert was shorter than I was but huskier. Mackenzie had curly hair and freckles. He was about my height. Like Anthony, they mouthed polite greetings.

One look and I knew all three. They were good at sports. They wore the right clothes. They had the right haircuts. They were full of whatever it is that makes you popular.

"We're playing my new video game," Anthony began, but his mother interrupted him.

"Let's turn that off now, boys," she said. "I've made a big pitcher of lemonade. Go out on the deck, and I'll bring it to you."

With some reluctance, Anthony left the computer and led the way outside. "I hear you live in the murder house," he said as we all sat down around a big table with a glass top.

I nodded, once again reminded that my house was famous all over town, even out here in Fair Oaks.

"It must be creepy," Mackenzie said.

"I'd hate to live there," Robert put in.

"And not just because of the murder," Anthony said. "You know who Logan's next-door neighbors are?"

The boys looked at him. "Who?" asked Mackenzie.

"Arthur Jenkins and his fruitcake grandmother!"

All three laughed and groaned and carried on. Rhoda chose that moment to appear with a tray. Setting down four frosty glasses of lemonade, she smiled. "Look at you all. Laughing like old friends already."

As soon as his mother left, Anthony said, "Arthur is the weirdest kid in Bealesville. How do you stand living next door to him?"

Here was my opportunity to turn my back on Arthur and make friends with Anthony, Robert, and Mackenzie. A few weeks ago, I would've jumped at the chance. But now I found myself remembering that guys like them never liked me. Sooner or later they'd dump me. Maybe I'd fumble the ball or strike out in a big game or say something dumb. They'd decide I was socially inept. A nerd. A creep. A weirdo like Arthur.

But Arthur—well, Arthur was Arthur. He didn't care about clothes or haircuts or striking out. He loved books and riding his hopeless old bike and doing interesting stuff. Best of all, he was never boring. Irritating, maybe, but not boring. And he lived right next door, not miles away in a big fancy house.

Before answering, I swallowed a mouthful of lemonade. Fresh squeezed, not made from a mix. It was so sweet, it made my jaw ache.

"Arthur's not bad," I said.

"You *like* Arthur Jenkins?" Anthony and his friends looked at me as if I'd just confessed to something totally gross, like ordering ice cream with olives and anchovies on top.

"Well, yeah, he's okay," I blundered on despite their incredulous stares. "In fact, we're trying to figure out who killed Mrs. Donaldson," I added, hoping they'd find that so interesting, they'd change their opinion of Arthur.

The three exchanged glances and started laughing. "It was probably Arthur's grandmother," Mackenzie said.

"She looks like an ax murderer," Robert added, snickering.

"I tell you seriously, Logan, you'd better not hang out with Arthur at school," Anthony said.

Mackenzie laughed. "It'll be you and Arthur . . . against the world."

The three stared at me, waiting to see if I'd change my mind about Arthur. But how could I? I remembered how sad he'd looked watching me ride off in Mom's car. Plus I knew full well these guys had no genuine interest in being friends with me. I was there because Anthony's mother, with some input from *my* mother, had invited me.

I shrugged and looked down at my running shoes, the same brand as theirs but not the same style. Not the *right* style.

Back in Richmond, I was used to hanging out around the edges of things. Here it seemed even the edges would be out of my reach. As Arthur Jenkins's sidekick, I was doomed to be way, way out there, on a distant planet of no interest to anyone.

"I hear your dad's the new art teacher at Beale High," Anthony said, mercifully changing the subject.

"Yeah."

"I guess that's why you live in Arthur's neighborhood," Mackenzie said.

I looked at him and frowned, not sure of the connection.

Robert sighed. "Teachers can't afford to live out here. Not on their salaries."

I looked from one boy to another. They sat back in their chairs, grinning, waiting to hear my reply. That was another thing about popular guys. Nothing I said would bother them. They knew they were my superiors. What was the use of trying to talk to them?

So I just shrugged and reached for my glass of lemonade.

Mackenzie put down his empty glass and got to his feet. "Anybody ready to finish that game?"

The other two followed him inside. Nobody asked if I wanted to play, so I stayed where I was and wished my mother would take me home. This had to be one of the worst mornings of my life.

15

U nfortunately, the day wasn't over. A few minutes later, Rhoda called down to announce lunch was ready.

The three guys ran upstairs ahead of me, pushing and shoving each other to see who'd get to the top first, laughing and joking in a mindless jock way.

Rhoda and Mom had set up lunch on the upper deck. A platter of roast beef sandwiches and turkey wraps sat in the middle of the table. A tin tub full of ice held enough sodas for twenty or thirty people. On the side were bowls of tossed salad, potato salad, and strawberries, as well as a plate of brownies.

If Arthur had seen all the food, he would have thought he'd died and gone to heaven. But he wasn't here. It was just me and three guys who had already decided I was a total loser.

We all sat down. Mom smiled happily at me. I knew she was thinking, "Isn't this more fun than hanging out with Arthur?" She saw what she wanted to see—me, Logan, making friends with popular guys—instead of the truth—me, Logan, having a miserable time with popular guys.

While the other boys laughed and joked, I ate my turkey wrap silently. It didn't taste nearly as good as it looked. Or maybe it was just me.

Every now and then I glanced at Mom, hoping she'd notice things weren't going as well as she'd hoped. But she was too busy yakking with Rhoda to notice I was miserable.

Suddenly, Rhoda turned to me with a big smile. "So, Logan," she said in her cheerful voice. "What sports do you play? Anthony, Robert, and Mackenzie have been playing soccer since they were born, practically. They're great in track, too. Anthony broke a record for the fifty-yard dash last year. And Mackenzie's a fantastic pole vaulter. Oh, and Robert—Robert, how could I leave you out? Wait till you see him throw that shot put thing. Unbelievable."

She raised her soda can to toast the boys. They bowed and grinned and jostled each other. As a result, Robert spilled his soda on my leg.

"Sorry, Lo," he said.

"So what sport, Logan? What position?" Rhoda persisted. "With those long legs, I bet you're a runner, too. Or maybe basketball's your thing? Mackenzie's really great on the court. Poetry in motion. High scorer almost every game."

"I don't do anything special," I admitted. "In fact, I, well, I—"

"In other words, your position is spectator," Anthony said.

Except for Mom and me, everyone laughed.

Rhoda turned to Mom. "My son has a fantastic sense of humor, doesn't he? So quick on the uptake. His grandfather thinks he's funny enough to be on TV."

Mom nodded, but she had her eye on me, as if she was finally beginning to realize lunch was not a big success.

Somehow I finished my wrap, ate some salad, and choked down a brownie. When Anthony led his friends downstairs to resume their game, no one invited me to go with them. Not that I wanted to.

Luckily, Mom and Rhoda were too busy cleaning up to notice me sitting alone in a corner of the living room, reading the only printed material I could find: this week's *TV Guide*.

Out in the kitchen, I heard Rhoda say, "You should encourage him to play a sport. It's the only way to survive middle school."

"Logan's not a natural athlete," Mom said. "Frankly, he'd rather read."

"A loner," Rhoda said as if she were pronouncing my death sentence.

"No, not a loner," Mom said quickly. "Just not a team player."

"Same thing," Rhoda said.

They moved out of hearing range, leaving me to imagine myself growing up to be a miserable failure, alone, friendless, unwanted.

At last, Mom came out of the kitchen, purse in hand, and I followed her and Rhoda to the car. The boys stayed downstairs. I could hear muffled explosions as the heroes fought the bad guys.

As I opened the car door, Rhoda gave me a pat on the back. "Anthony and his friends just can't get enough of that silly game. Maybe you should take it up yourself." She paused. "That or basketball. You'll be amazed at the difference sports make in your life."

"Yeah." I eased into the car.

Before I could close the door, Rhoda added, "Don't keep your nose in a book. You won't make friends that way."

This time I didn't say anything, but I did try to smile—a poor effort, I'm sure.

Mom thanked Rhoda for a lovely lunch and promised to call her soon. At last we were backing down the long driveway, waving to Rhoda, saying goodbye.

We hadn't gone more than a block when Mom said, "You didn't even try, did you?"

"Mom, I don't have anything in common with guys like that."

She frowned at the big houses we were passing. "I simply don't understand you, Logan."

I didn't answer.

"I thought you'd have fun, I thought you'd make friends, I thought—"

"Well, you thought wrong."

And that was that, as far as conversation was concerned. We rode home in silence. Not the comfortable kind, either. Mom was mad, and I was mad. Worse yet, she was disappointed, which made me feel guilty for letting her down.

When we pulled into the driveway, Mom said, "I'm sorry today wasn't more fun for you, Logan." She hesitated a moment. "But you have to make an effort. We've been invited to Rhoda's for a party on Saturday. Maybe this time you and Anthony—"

"Mom," I interrupted, "it won't matter how hard I try. Kids like Anthony hate kids like me."

"Just try—please?" Mom looked at me with worried eyes. "Try, Logan. That's all I ask."

My eyes strayed to Arthur's house. The grass was a foot taller than ours, and a shutter hung crookedly at an upstairs window. For the first time I realized how sad his house looked, especially now that Johnny and Dad had almost finished painting ours and whipping the lawn into shape.

Mom sighed. "If you don't like Anthony, find someone you do like. A nice boy from a good home. Not . . ."

She didn't need to finish the sentence. We both knew what she meant. Someone who's popular, plays sports, gets good grades, fits in. Someone whose father makes big bucks. Someone who lives in a fancy house.

Disconsolately, I followed Mom inside, achingly aware of Arthur's eyes watching me from somewhere.

I spent the rest of the day moping around the house and getting in everyone's way. Now and then I glanced out a window and saw Arthur reading on his front porch or tinkering with the Raleigh in his back yard. Mrs. Jenkins puttered around in her flower garden, weeding and pruning, singing old songs in a low monotone. May tagged along behind her, trying to help. I guessed Violet was at work, and Danny was with his friends.

Neither Mrs. Jenkins nor Arthur looked at our house. Mom had most likely offended both of them. That made me even sadder.

I put food out for Bear the way I always did, but he

seemed to be avoiding us, too. Mom didn't miss him, but Dad mentioned him several times. Even asked if I'd filled his bowl. Wordlessly, I pointed to the untouched kibble.

The next morning, neither Arthur nor Bear showed up at breakfast time. I spent a long, boring day tagging along with Mom to a big shopping outlet about twenty miles away. She insisted on buying me shirts and shorts like the ones Anthony and his friends wore. She made me get a haircut like theirs. And shoes like theirs. At last, she let my buy some science fiction paperbacks at a huge place called Book Warehouse. That was the only good part of the day. Except lunch.

The next day, I put on my Anthony clothes, and Mom and I drove all the way to Washington, D.C. It was the hottest day of the entire summer—ninety-nine degrees, with humidity so thick you could hardly breathe. And here Mom and I were, dragging ourselves from one air-conditioned museum to the next. Air and Space, Natural History, American History, American Indian, National Gallery of Art. After a while, we were so exhausted, we collapsed on a black leather sofa and stared at a seascape by Winslow Homer. The cool green water looked real enough to jump into—except for the sharks swimming around the boat. They reminded me of Silas and Billy.

I sat there in the museum, dressed like a fake friend of Anthony, and wondered if Silas had found the evidence that revealed the killer's name. His own, probably.

16

The day of Rhoda's party was sunny and warm but not hot. Mom made sure I had on one of my Anthony outfits—white polo shirt, khaki pants, new running shoes, tan socks, brown belt. I was surprised she didn't insist on checking my underwear as well.

When she was satisfied with my clothes, she combed my hair as if I were six years old. It felt like the first day of school—only worse.

Done with me, Mom started on Dad. Why hadn't he gotten a haircut like she'd told him to? Surely he wasn't wearing his faded SAVE THE WHALES T-shirt? "And those jeans," she said. "They have paint spattered all over them."

Dad said, "I'm an art teacher—why shouldn't I wear these jeans? And what's wrong with my shirt?"

"The party's dressy-casual." She smoothed the skirt of a black and white print sundress she'd bought on our outlet shopping trip. "At the very least, that means a nice polo shirt and khaki pants."

"You know I don't want to go to this party," Dad said. "What am I supposed to say to a bunch of businessmen and lawyers? They're probably all Republicans or Libertarians or—"

"Forget politics for once!" Mom's voice rose. "If you can't think of me, think of your son. Logan needs to make a good impression on people. I want people to see he comes from a good family."

Dad shot me a look, and I rolled my eyes, signaling I was just as unhappy as he was.

"Just go upstairs and put on a nice shirt," Mom begged him, "and a pair of slacks. And take those sandals off!"

"You mean I can go barefoot?"

"You know what I mean!" Mom was getting close to the explosion point. Next, she'd start on Dad's hippie past and his low salary and the dumpy house we lived in. Before I knew it, they'd be divorced and I'd have to pick which one to live with. Dad, probably. I had more in common with him. My belly twisted.

"Sorry. They'll have to take me as I am." Dad walked outside and opened the car door. "Are you coming?"

Red-faced, Mom flounced across the yard. "Come on, Logan," she said in an I'm-not-taking-any-more-of-this voice.

Out of habit, I glanced at Arthur's house. He was sitting on the front steps reading a picture book to May. Mrs. Jenkins was watering her flowers. Bear dozed in a patch of dirt beside the porch. There was no sign of Violet or Danny.

Not one of them looked at me. Not even Bear. My belly cramped harder.

The ride to Fair Oaks was very quiet. Which was better than an argument. Or maybe not. Dad stuck a CD of an old blues singer into the car's player. "I'm a good man, but I'm a poor man," he sang along with Skip James. "You can understand."

Mom huffed a loud sigh and stared out her window at the green lawns of Fair Oaks. "You and Skip James," she muttered.

Thanks to the wardrobe argument, the party was in full swing when we arrived. People spilled over the decks and patios and onto the lawn. As Mom had predicted, the men were wearing polo shirts in shades of red and blue and green and yellow neatly tucked into the Dockers pants Dad hated.

Obviously, he didn't blend in, but Mom did. Rhoda DiSilvio was wearing a sundress just like hers, which for some reason seemed to upset both of them.

"Go and mingle." Mom gave me a little push toward a group of kids my age.

"Look who's here." Anthony laughed. "Arthur's buddy, Logan."

They all stared at me as if I had the plague—the Arthur plague, I guessed.

The girls started to giggle. The prettiest one shoved another girl toward me. "Sandy has a crush on Arthur," she said. "She wants you to tell him he's the cutest boy in Bealesville."

"I do not!" Sandy glared at me as if it was all my fault that everyone was laughing. "I hate Arthur! He's a total weirdo!"

Suddenly, a hand touched my shoulder, and I turned to see Nina. Looking more beautiful than ever, she was wearing a strapless blue and white dress, and her hair hung down in perfect shiny waves.

"Logan," she said with a smile. "I haven't seen you for a while."

Before I knew it, she was leading me away, rescuing me from Anthony and his friends. Instead of being grateful, I shrugged her hand off my shoulder. Beautiful or not, she wasn't the person I'd thought she was. She'd talked to Silas, she'd believed his lies, she'd blabbed to my mother, she'd messed up my friendship with Arthur.

"Is something wrong?" Nina asked. She stood so close I could smell her perfume, fresh and sweet, like summer itself.

I stepped away from her. "Why did you tell Mom those lies about the library? Arthur's the only friend I have in this stupid town. Now, thanks to you, I can't hang out with him anymore. What's with you and Silas and Billy, anyway? Why would you—"

Nina put her hand on my shoulder again to calm me down. "I didn't realize your mother would feel that strongly about what I said." She hesitated. "But I honestly think you'd be better off without Arthur. He's not really your type, Logan."

I shrugged her hand away as it were an annoying bug or something. She obviously didn't know any more about my type than Mom did.

But before I could say anything, a tall, adult version of Anthony joined us. He was neatly dressed in an expensive green polo shirt and pressed khaki trousers. Blown-dry hair, too, and a fancy watch on a big silver band.

A smile lit Nina's face. "Oh, Richard," she said, "have you met Logan Forbes? His family bought the Donaldson house."

The man smiled a tooth-baring grin and shook my hand so firmly it hurt. "I'm Anthony's dad," he said. "I was just talking to your father. Interesting fellow. Knows a lot about art."

"Yeah," I said, "he *teaches* art."

As I extricated my hand from Mr. DiSilvio's bone-crunching grasp, I wondered what Dad thought of this guy, strutting around like the lord of the manor. I figured he and my father had no more in common than Anthony and I did—which would rile Mom, who seemed to hope that this party was the beginning of a round of socializing with people like the DiSilvios.

"So how do you like Bealesville?" he asked me.

"It's okay."

He studied me for a moment. His eyes were an odd shade of yellow green, speckled like a lizard's, and rimmed in black. Nina stood beside him, sipping her wine. Suddenly uncomfortable, I looked away from the two of them and searched for a friendly face. All I saw was Anthony and his gang.

"I hear you and the Jenkins boy have gotten interested in Mrs. Donaldson's death," Mr. DiSilvio said, and now his smile was patronizing.

I glanced at Nina, sure she was the one who'd told him, but she ignored the accusation in my eyes.

"A woman murdered in your house," he went on, still smiling. "Her killer never caught. It sounds like a crime for the Hardy Boys to solve."

The sarcasm in his voice was impossible to miss. Forcing myself to look him in the eye, I said, "I grew out of the Hardy Boys a long time ago."

"I'm glad to hear it." Mr. DiSilvio took a sip of wine and smiled at Nina, including her in his little joke. Then he turned back to me.

"Nina tells me she saw you and Arthur in the Magic Forest. You know that's my property, don't you? 'No trespassing' means no trespassing. Right?" He took another sip of wine. "I don't want you or the Jenkins kid on my property. You could fall or hurt yourself. You think I want your parents suing me?"

"Nina was trespassing, too," I said.

"Don't be such a smart mouth," he said. "I gave Nina permission to photograph the park for her newspaper story. She's a responsible adult with too much sense to fall in a hole and break her leg."

While we'd been talking, the long summer day had slowly ended. Shadows from trees slanted darkly across the grass. The other guests, including Anthony and his friends, were strolling toward the patio, where the food waited.

Increasingly uneasy, I edged away from the two grown-ups. "I smell hamburgers."

"Steak," Mr. DiSilvio corrected. "U.S. Prime."

With her hand on my arm, Nina began walking up the sloping lawn. "If I know Rhoda," she said to Mr. DiSilvio, "it will be delicious."

"She's having the food catered by the Wandering Gourmets," Mr. DiSilvio said. "They're based in Richmond. Absolutely the best, unequaled—even in D.C."

He waved a hand at the lawn, the flowers, the big house, the guests. "Only the best," he boasted, "that's what I provide for my family and friends."

Nina smiled. "It's a lovely party. I appreciate your invitation."

He stroked her arm lightly and leaned closer. "I'm glad you're here."

"I wouldn't have missed it," Nina said.

At the edge of the patio, Mr. DiSilvio paused and gave me a long look, as if he was sizing me or up or something. I tried to meet his eyes, but he made me so nervous, I ended up scanning the crowd for Mom or Dad, the only people here I felt comfortable with.

"Rhoda told me you're not interested in sports," he said. "But being on the soccer team would help you fit in with other kids. You don't want to start middle school with no friends."

"I'm not good at sports." I shot an angry look at Nina. *I used to have a friend,* I thought, *until you messed everything up with your lies.*

"Anybody can be good if he tries," Mr. DiSilvio said. "You just have to have the right attitude."

Sneering mentally at his platitudes, I said, "I'm better at chess and stuff like that."

"A brain, huh?" Mr. DiSilvio laughed and gave me a playful cuff on the arm. "Well, don't get too smart for your own good."

Still smiling as if it was all a joke, Mr. DiSilvio excused himself. "It's time for me to be a good host and make sure my guests are enjoying themselves."

I watched him join a group of men clustered around the bar, drinking and talking loudly about baseball. To my surprise, Johnny was serving. He was so spiffed up, I almost didn't recognize him. I glanced around for Billy, but I didn't see him. Even if you dressed him in designer clothes, he'd still look like a bum.

Nina maneuvered me toward a table covered with food. She speared a jumbo shrimp with a toothpick and dipped it in some kind of pink sauce. "The tall man next to Richard is a state representative," she told me. "The man beside him is the county executive. Lawyers, planners, a few commissioners. the chief of police, and so on. All of them powers in the community."

"I didn't know you were friends with the DiSilvios," I said.

"I met Richard when I interviewed him about Mrs. Donaldson." Nina speared another shrimp and ate it. "Since he was the park's accountant, I wondered if he thought she embezzled the money."

Interested in spite of myself, I asked, "What did he say?"

"He's convinced she took the money, but it pained him to admit it." Nina sighed. "Richard trusted Myrtle Donaldson. He thought she was a loyal employee. A nice woman, a good person."

"What about her murder?"

"In Richard's opinion, she was murdered by someone who believed she'd hidden the stolen money in her house." Nina shrugged. "That's what the police think, too."

I gripped my soda can and looked her in the eye. "It's not what Arthur's grandmother thinks. She—"

"Oh, for heaven's sakes, Logan. You can't take that

woman seriously. She has an opinion about everything. And not one of them has any basis in fact."

"I'd take her word over yours any day." I was mad now. "*She'd* never tell lies to my mother. *She'd* never sneak around with Billy and Silas. *She'd* never come to a party like this with all these phony people. *She'd* never talk about you behind your back!"

"You really are angry with me, aren't you?"

"Yes," I almost shouted. "I don't like you, and I don't trust you. And I'd never tell you anything Arthur and I know!"

Nina seized my shoulders and shoved her face so close to mine I could smell the shrimp she'd just eaten. "Listen to me, Logan. You're a nice kid and I don't want—" She broke off suddenly and veered in a different direction. "Leave crime solving to the police. Forget about Mrs. Donaldson. Stay away from the Magic Forest. You and Arthur both. Those ruins are in bad shape. You could get hurt playing there."

She bit into a small sandwich. "Take Richard's advice. Join a soccer team, make friends when school starts."

"I hate sports," I shouted. "And I *had* a friend until you ruined everything."

Nina waved her hand impatiently. "Well, join something else, then. A book club, a science club, a chess team. Just stop meddling. Stay away from—" She broke off when Rhoda appeared at her side.

"Nina, I've been looking everywhere for you," Rhoda said. "I want you to meet someone." Without a word or even a look at me, she swept Nina away.

Left alone, I wandered around the party looking for my

parents. The guests certainly seemed to be enjoying themselves, drinking, eating, laughing, talking. I caught a glimpse of Johnny leaning across the bar, chatting with some guests. On the lawn, just beyond the reach of lights, Anthony and his friends were playing a rough game of soccer. The girls had gathered on the sidelines to cheer them on. Nina, Mr. DiSilvio, and Rhoda were surrounded by important-looking people.

I finally found my mother talking to a stylish woman about paint. "Try Ralph Lauren's earth tones," she told Mom. "They're *fabulous*."

Tugging Mom's arm to get her attention, I whined, "My stomach hurts. Can we go home?"

"Drink a soda fast, honey," the woman said. "It's the best cure I know for an upset stomach."

If Dad hadn't joined us, I would have been stuck at the party for hours. "Let's get out of here," he said. "I'm tired of socializing."

I slipped an arm around Dad's waist and leaned my head against his chest. "Me, too."

Mom and the woman parted with a hug and a promise to meet for lunch soon. We found Rhoda and said our goodbyes and our thank-yous.

As we headed toward our car, Nina called after me, "Behave yourself, Logan."

Mom laughed. "I'll see that he does," she promised.

At last we got into the only car in the neighborhood more than a year old and worth less than fifty thousand dollars. And drove away.

"Don't ever drag me to something like that again," Dad

muttered to Mom. "Bores and Philistines and conservatives of the worst kind."

Mom sighed. "I thought it was a lovely party."

"I'm with Dad." I patted his shoulder. "That was absolutely the worst party I've ever gone to."

"Except for the food," Dad said. "Too bad we couldn't have ordered take-away."

To Mom's annoyance, we both laughed. It was a guy moment, a bonding thing, and I was happy when Dad reached back to tousle my hair.

17

L ate that night, when I was sure Mom and Dad were asleep, I aimed my flashlight at Arthur's window. It took a lot of probing, beaming the light here and there, making it flit through the dark like a demented firefly, but I had to see him.

Finally, Arthur came to the window and stared across the space between us. "What do *you* want?" he asked in a grumpy voice.

"We've got to talk. Can you sneak outside and meet me?"

He nodded and disappeared. As quietly as possible, I crept downstairs and slipped out into the summer night. It was still hot. Thunder rumbled far away, and reddish heat lightning flickered across the dark sky. It was like looking at a battle being fought just over the horizon, the sky lit with rockets and the ground reverberating with artillery fire.

Arthur was waiting for me under a tree, arms folded across his skinny chest. Bear sat beside him, scratching fleas. "What do we have to talk about?" Arthur asked sarcastically. "Now that you're friends with Anthony?"

"I *hate* Anthony. Blame Mom, blame Nina, but don't blame me."

"What's Nina got to do with it?"

"Plenty." I told him about her phone call to Mom, leaving out what she'd said about his being an unsuitable friend. I let my mother take the blame for that.

"But how did Nina know what happened in the library?" Arthur asked.

"*Silas,*" I said. "Silas told her. That's why he didn't follow us to the graveyard. He stopped to talk to her."

For once I was ahead of Arthur.

"How would *they* know each other?" he asked, his face puzzled.

"Maybe she interviewed him about the murder," I said. "After all, he was a suspect for a while."

Arthur nodded. "She knows Billy and Johnny—why not Silas, too?"

"Listen," I said, "there's more. Mom made Dad and me go to this disgusting party at the DiSilvios' house. Nina was there. She started talking to me, being all friendly and stuff. Then Mr. DiSilvio came over and joined in. He actually told me I should join a soccer team."

When Arthur laughed, I knew everything was all right and we were friends again.

"All of a sudden," I went on, "Mr. DiSilvio dropped the chummy act and told me to stay away from the Magic Forest—he owns the land, it's private property, it's dangerous, etc., etc., etc. He kept grinning, but I swear he was threatening me."

"Nina, Silas, Billy, Johnny, and now Mr. DiSilvio," Arthur said. "How does *he* fit in?"

I'd been asking myself the same question, but I shook my head, just as mystified as Arthur.

We sat under the tree for a while and listened to the thunder mutter a long way away. All around us, hidden in the dark leaves, the cicadas buzzed their monotonous serenade.

"Did you know Danny's living with Silas?" Arthur asked after a while.

"I wondered why I hadn't seen him."

Arthur picked up a stone and tossed it at our garbage can. He missed by a mile. "He wanted to take Bear, but Silas wouldn't let him."

The dog heard his name and wagged his tail. I reached out and patted his head. "Good dog," I whispered. "You're too smart to go with Danny."

"You'd think Violet would be glad to be rid of him," Arthur continued, "but she mopes around all day and cries all night. Then May cries. It's driving me nuts."

"Have you talked to Violet about the finding game?" I asked.

"I haven't had a chance, what with Danny going off with Silas, and her being all sad and weepy."

Arthur picked up another stone and aimed again at the garbage can. This time he actually hit it with a loud clang. Bear started barking. Dad came to the window and shouted, "Shut up, Bear!"

Arthur and I froze in the shadows under the tree. Bear

snorted and lay back down. Without seeing us, Dad went back to bed.

"It's better when you miss," I told him.

"I didn't think it would make so much noise." Arthur yawned and stood up. "I got to go, but let's talk to Violet tomorrow."

Glad the darkness hid my face, I said, "This is really embarrassing, but Mom won't let me go to your house anymore—thanks to Nina and her lies."

"That Nina." Arthur scowled. "How about meeting at the library around ten? If Mrs. Jones lets us in, that is."

"Mom made me give back the map and apologize to Mrs. Bailey and Mrs. Jones," I said. "They didn't act mad or anything."

With a sigh, Arthur walked off into the darkness. Bear lumbered after him, his tags jingling.

All alone, I slipped silently into the murder house.

The next morning, I hopped on my bike and sped away before Mom had a chance to stop me. When I got to the library, I saw Arthur's old Raleigh lying on the sidewalk. I locked mine to the bike rack and went inside. A new poster caught my eye. In great big letters it said: PROTEST THE DESTRUCTION OF THE MAGIC FOREST! And below that, in slightly smaller print, was this: "Bulldozers go into action at 8 A.M. Tuesday August 25. Help us stop them!" Near the bottom of the poster it said: "Come as your favorite nursery rhyme characters. *Be There at Sunrise!*"

A young woman standing nearby gave me a big smile. "I'm going dressed as Mama Bear," she said. "My husband's

Papa Bear, and our little boy is Baby Bear. I made the costumes for Halloween last year."

"Great," I said. "That's really great." *A little weird*, I thought, *but definitely interesting.*

"Meet us in the park tomorrow. My family will be there at four A.M., but most people won't arrive until six or seven." She smiled. "Bring all your friends—the more we have, the better."

I nodded, and she walked off with an armload of books. I didn't tell her that bringing all my friends meant exactly one person.

Arthur sat at a table in the children's room. Violet was with him. May sat between them, playing with the plastic gingerbread men. The copy of the note and one of the Magic Forest maps lay beside Violet's elbow.

"She knows what the note means," Arthur whispered. "She figured it out last night."

Violet glanced around the library. Not far away, Mrs. Bunions browsed through a rack of romance paperbacks. Near her, a man sat in the reference area, his face hidden behind a newspaper. Several other adults wandered among the shelves, looking for books.

"When I was little," Violet said in a low voice, "Mom used to take me to the Magic Forest while she worked. She let me play anywhere I liked, but I never went near the Witch's Hut—I was really scared of her."

Arthur turned to me to explain. "The witch was life-size. She had a green face and a long nose, and she was really ugly. Hideous, in fact. Every ten minutes or so, she'd pop out of the hut door, wave her arms, and cackle. I thought she was a real live crazy woman. You wouldn't believe the nightmares I had about her escaping from the hut and chasing me."

Violet shuddered. "I thought the same thing." She picked up one of the little plastic gingerbread men. "There was a fence made of twelve wooden gingerbread men like these. They stood in a row, holding hands along the path leading to the witch's door. They were kind of cute and kind of scary at the same time. But they didn't frighten me the way the witch did."

She smiled at May. "When I was around your age," she went on, "Mom decided I was too big to be scared of a silly old fake witch. One day, she told me she'd thought of a game to play. To make me brave."

May looked up at Violet. "I'm not very brave. I'm scared of spiders and spooky things in the dark and witches under my bed and wolves in my closet."

I felt like saying I wasn't very brave, either, but I kept my mouth shut and waited for Violet to go on with her story.

"At lunchtime," Violet said, "Mom and I ate our sandwiches on a bench near the path to the Witch's Hut. One day after we'd eaten, she showed me a little plastic gingerbread man."

"Like these?" May toyed with the little men. She'd put them in a circle, so each one had a hand to hold.

Violet nodded. "Mom walked over to the first gingerbread man, the one farthest from the hut. She hid the plastic figure in the grass near it. If I could find it, she said I could keep it—a prize for being brave."

May leaned against her mother's side. "That sounds easy."

"It was," Violet said. "All I had to do was poke around in

the grass at the feet of the first gingerbread man and find my prize. I was nowhere near the hut, so I wasn't scared."

"What color was it?" May asked. "Red? Green? Yellow?" She held up the little men one at a time.

Violet smiled at May. "I think it was red."

May slid a red man across the table to her mother. "There's your prize, Mommy."

Violet swept the little man into the palm of her hand. "The next day," she went on, "Mom hid a blue man near the second gingerbread man. The day after that, she hid a green one near the third gingerbread man."

"Your mommy was mean to make you go closer and closer to the hut," May said.

Violet shook her head. "No, honey, she was trying to show me there was nothing to be scared of."

Turning to Arthur and me, she went on, "Some days, I didn't win a prize because I was too scared. I'd have to try again the next day."

While Violet talked, May had counted the gingerbread men. "Eleven!" she said. "Did you get them all?"

Violet shook her head. "Mom hid the twelfth one in front of the last gingerbread man—right next to the witch's doorstep. Just as I got close, the hut door flew open and out came the witch, waving her arms and cackling. As much as I wanted the last little man, I ran to Mom, bawling my head off. I never went near the hut again."

She paused to smooth May's hair out of her eyes. "After a while, I got too old for the Magic Forest. I forgot about the finding game and the witch."

"Maybe he's still there," May said. "We could go and look for him."

"It's too late now," Violet said. "I'd never find him. The whole park is a jungle of weeds and kudzu vines. I wouldn't know where to look."

"The hut is right here." Arthur stabbed the map with his finger. "I know we can find it!"

Violet stared at him. "Find what, Arthur? A tumbledown shack, a little plastic man?"

"The briefcase!" Arthur was so excited he almost shouted. Mrs. Bunions turned, her finger to her mouth to shush us, but the man with the paper kept on reading as if he hadn't heard a thing.

"Don't you see?" He lowered his voice. "It has to be buried near the Witch's Hut."

"Do you really think it's still there?" Violet whispered.

"Yes, but not for much longer," Arthur said. "Once the bulldozers destroy the place, the briefcase, the money, and the evidence will be gone forever, and we'll never know who killed your mother."

"Suppose Silas already has it," I said. "He's got the note, he's got the map."

"Yes, but Violet's the only one who knows about the finding game. And she hasn't told Silas." He swung toward Violet. "Right?"

Violet nodded. "He might have the note, but he'll never figure it out."

Arthur jumped to his feet, earning another sharp look from Mrs. Bunions. "We've got to go to the Magic Forest right now!" He headed toward the door, expecting us all to rush after him.

"But, Arthur," Violet said, "I have to be at work in an hour."

"Can't you call in sick or something?"

"If I lose any more time, they'll fire me. And I can't afford—"

"When do you get off work?" Arthur interrupted.

"About ten thirty tonight, but—"

"We'll meet you at Wal-Mart," Arthur said. "And you can drive us to the park."

Violet hesitated. "Do we have to go there in the dark? Can't we wait until my day off or something?"

"The bulldozers are coming to demolish the place tomorrow," Arthur said. "It's tonight . . . or never."

The disgustingly wimpy part of me wanted to say, "*Never. Let it be never.*" But instead I said, "You don't have to come with us, Violet. We can find it without you. "

"I want to be there," she said in a low voice. "I owe it to my mother."

"Can I come, too?" May asked.

Violet hugged her. "Absolutely not. Your bedtime is seven thirty."

When May started to protest, Violet stacked up a pile of picture books. "Mrs. Jenkins can read these to you tonight."

"All of them?" May asked.

"That's up to Mrs. Jenkins." Violet gave her another hug and kissed her forehead. "Be a good girl tonight, and I'll treat you to ice cream tomorrow."

After Violet checked out her books, Arthur and I followed her and May out of the library and into the blazing heat of the August morning. As they drove away, I found myself wishing I could go to bed with a stack of books instead of traipsing around the Magic Forest looking for something we'd probably never find. And maybe running into someone we didn't want to meet in a dark place.

"I sure could use a nice cold soda," Arthur said. "Do you have any money?"

I had enough to buy one can of root beer at the rundown gas station on Laurel Avenue. In the park across the street, I drank half and passed the can to Arthur. Pigeons ambled around in circles, cooing to themselves in sad voices, and sparrows hopped here and there, picking crumbs out of cracks in the pavement.

With my head tipped back, I gazed across the dusty crabgrass at a granite pedestal topped by a life-size bronze statue of the town's founder, Robert Arthur Beale, 1841–1913. Shoulders splattered with bird droppings, he stood tall and gazed into the distance, most likely envisioning a city of the future, a place of real significance—not a little backwater town like Bealesville.

On a bench across from ours, two old men slumped side by side, just like Arthur and me. If we stayed in Bealesville long enough, we'd be sitting here when we were old, complaining about the heat and the cost of living, just like them.

Suddenly, a shadow slanted across my feet. I looked up to see Mr. DiSilvio standing in front of me, his back to the sun. "Well, hello, Logan," he said, flashing his white teeth in a big Hollywood smile.

"Oh—um—hi," I stammered, going from relaxed to tense in about one second. That was how the man affected me. Desperate for something to say, I asked, "Have you met Arthur Jenkins?"

Mr. DiSilvio gave Arthur the same fake smile. "I've heard a lot about you from Anthony."

He stuck out his hand, and Arthur shook it. Arthur's face was red, and I guessed he was thinking about the sorts of things Anthony must have told his father.

"Didn't I just see you in the library?" Mr. DiSilvio asked.

Arthur and I looked at each other, not sure what to say. Mr. DiSilvio must have been the man reading the paper. The man we'd barely noticed. The man sitting close enough to hear every word we'd said.

Without waiting for us to reply, Mr. DiSilvio slipped his hands into his pockets, jingling his coins and keys. "I always spend an hour or so there in the morning," he went on, "browsing through *The Wall Street Journal*. It's a pleasant way to start the day."

I slunk a little lower on the bench and wished he would go away. He had a way of making me feel stupid, tongue-tied, itchy with heat and sweat and embarrassment.

"I couldn't help overhearing what you said about going to the Magic Forest tonight." Mr. DiSilvio shook his head. "Despite the rumors, there's no money buried there. Mrs. Donaldson took the secret of its whereabouts to the grave."

The sun was in my eyes, and I had to squint to see him

clearly. "Frankly," he went on, "the park's a dangerous place, especially after dark. You could trip over a log, injure yourself, maybe break a leg. The buildings aren't safe, either. The county condemned the whole place. Surely you've noticed the big red signs posted everywhere. Not to mention the 'no trespassing' signs." He frowned. "I'm tempted to call your parents and tell them what you're up to. As the owner, I'd feel responsible if anything happened to you boys."

I found myself agreeing. The park *was* dangerous. Spooky. Deserted. Overgrown with vines and weeds. A weird and lonely place full of grotesque statues and dilapidated buildings. The haunt of Jarmons and Phelpses and who knew who else. I didn't want to go to there. Not in the daytime. And certainly not in the nighttime.

Mr. DiSilvio smiled at me approvingly. "This is real life, kids," he said, "not a TV thriller."

I glanced at Arthur, expecting him to shoot off his big mouth. Eyes slitted against the sun, he stared up at Mr. DiSilvio. To my surprise, he nodded his head. "We were just kidding around," he said. "I'd be scared to go out there after dark. Even in the daytime it's way too creepy."

Turning to me, he added, "Let's just forget the whole thing, Logan. Stay home, watch videos at my house or something. I just rented a cool Japanese horror movie."

"That's a great idea," I said, limp with relief. Saved—I was saved. Instead of meeting some horrible end in the Magic Forest, I'd have a chance to grow up after all.

"Now you're making sense," Mr. DiSilvio said. Glancing at his watch, he added, "Nice to see you, boys. Take care."

As he walked away, I sighed happily. "I didn't think you'd give in like that. I expected you to—"

Arthur stared at me, obviously puzzled. "What makes you think I gave in?"

"Well . . . you said we'd stay home, didn't you? And watch videos?"

"Logan, did you take a stupid pill instead of a vitamin this morning?"

My heart dropped with a cold thud from my chest to my stomach. "You mean we're still going?"

"How else can we get the briefcase and clear Mrs. Donaldson's name?" he looked at me closely. "Are you wimping out on me?"

I shrugged. "Of course not. It's just that—"

"It's just that you're scared." Arthur tossed the soda can into a trash basket and grabbed his bike. "I only said that to keep him from calling your mother. I hope it worked."

I pedaled after Arthur silently. I should have known what he was up to.

We split up at the corner so my mother wouldn't see us together. Before he rode away, Arthur said, "There's something about DiSilvio, something fake and sly and, and . . ." His voice trailed off. For once he couldn't find the right word.

But I knew exactly what he meant.

18

After a long afternoon of reading and watching TV, I went to bed around nine, my usual time. I had to wait until dark—full dark—to risk sneaking out. When I thought it was safe, I slid the screen up and climbed out my window onto the front porch roof. Quietly, very quietly, I crept to the edge and climbed down the pine tree beside the house. I felt like a kid in a book running away from home.

I peeked through the living room window. Mom and Dad sat side by side on the couch watching an old movie. Suddenly, I felt this huge tide of sentimentality rush over me. There they were, totally unaware that their one and only child was about to risk his life on a dangerous mission. What if I never returned? Picturing their sorrow almost made me cry. Their son, their little boy—lost forever in a jungle of kudzu.

Just as I was about to climb back up the tree, I heard a low whistle from Arthur's yard. It was too late to back out. I had to go.

Quietly, I wheeled my bike out of the garage. With Bear

trotting beside us, Arthur and I rode away into the night. Automobile headlights shone in our faces, almost blinding us. A man yelled at us for riding without lights. I guess it didn't help that we were both wearing dark clothes.

It took us longer than we'd thought to get to Wal-Mart. When we finally arrived, a little after eleven, the huge neon sign was out and the parking lot was dark and spooky in the moonlight.

"That's Violet's old Ford." Arthur pedaled toward the only car in the lot. "Sorry we're late," he called out.

No one answered. We looked inside. The car was empty.

"Where is she?" I asked.

We went to the store and peered through the glass doors. A dim security light lit the interior. It was obvious everyone had left.

Arthur frowned. "Something's wrong. I feel it in my bones."

I felt it, too, a sort of cold dread rising from the soles of my feet to the top of my head. "What should we do?"

Before Arthur could come up with an answer, a shadowy figure stepped out from behind a row of Wal-Mart Dumpsters. I didn't know who it was, nor was I about to hang around and find out.

With adrenaline pumping through me, I started pedaling toward the highway and home. Arthur sped past me. But not Bear. Tail wagging, the dog ran toward the Dumpsters.

"Come back here!" somebody yelled at us.

"It's Danny." Arthur braked to a screeching stop, and I swerved to miss hitting him.

The two of us watched as Danny pedaled toward us on his old bike. "What are you doing here?" he hollered.

"What are *you* doing here?" Arthur asked.

Danny pulled up beside us. "Looking for my mother," he said. Even though he kept his head down, I could see bruises on his face. One eye was swollen shut.

"What happened to you?" Arthur asked.

Danny shrugged. "None of your business, weirdo."

"Your mother's not here," I said in an effort to change the subject.

Danny looked at me scornfully. "Duh."

"We were supposed to meet her after she got off work," I went on.

"My dad beat you to it," Danny muttered.

"She's with *Silas?*" Arthur asked.

Danny gripped his bike's handlebars so tightly, his knuckles turned white. "Looks like it."

"Why would she go anywhere with him? She hates Silas."

"He has a way of making you do what he says." Apparently unaware of what he was doing, Danny touched his eye.

Arthur winced. "But you and your dad—"

"Don't say anything else about him. He don't deserve to be a dad or a husband or anything else. I wish they'd kept him in jail. I wish I never had to see him again in my whole life!" With that, Danny bent over Bear and rubbed his face in the dog's fur. "Good old Bear," he whispered. "Best old dog in the world."

Arthur and I glanced at each other. Neither of us knew

what to say or what to do. And we were scared. Scared for Violet, mainly, but also for Danny, who seemed to be crying, even though he couldn't be, not really. But still . . .

Finally, Arthur said, "He won't hurt Violet, will he?"

"What do *you* think?" The old Danny was back in control, sneer and all.

"Where did he take her?" Arthur asked.

"The Magic Forest, idiot. Where else? He thinks she knows where that money is." Danny frowned at his mother's empty car. "I came out here to warn her, but he got her first."

He sped off on his bike. When he saw us following him, he yelled, "Get out of here. Go home. You'll just mess everything up!"

But nothing could stop Arthur. Ignoring Danny, he headed down the highway right behind him. I rode after them, and Bear ran with me.

From the top of the hill, we stared down at the Magic Forest's parking lot. Except for a line of bulldozers waiting to roar into action the next day, it was empty.

Danny scowled at Arthur and me. "I told you not to come with me," he said.

Arthur shrugged. "Logan and I were supposed to meet your mother and drive out here with her."

"My mother wouldn't go anywhere with you jerks."

"Your mother's a nice person—" I began.

"A lot nicer than you," Arthur interrupted. Danny raised his fist, and Arthur stepped back. "Anyway," he went on, "we're here, and we're not leaving until we find Violet."

Pushing off with one foot, Danny sped down the hill. "If you get in trouble, don't expect no help from me," he yelled over his shoulder.

"Charming," Arthur muttered.

With Bear behind us, we caught up with Danny at the bottom of the hill. Avoiding the main gate, we followed the fence into the woods, stowed our bikes, and crawled through a hole in the fence.

If the Magic Forest was scary in the daylight, it was truly terrifying in the dark. All around us kudzu lifted and fell in the breeze, sighing as if it were a living, breathing creature, a shape changer. Now it was a monster, now an ogre, now a long-armed witch, always menacing, never benign, never still. Shadows shifted, darkened, lightened, grew, shrank. Leaves murmured like ghosts whispering to each other of death and decay.

With the help of a flashlight, Arthur studied the map. Bear cocked his head to the side and watched us, tail wagging, tongue lolling, eager to do whatever it was we were going to do.

Shoving me aside, Danny peered over Arthur's shoulder. "You think you know where it's at?" he asked.

Arthur nodded. "The first thing we need to do is find the right path. I figure it's the one that goes past the Old Woman's Shoe." He studied the map and looked around. "It should be over there somewhere, not far from Willie the Whale."

Thanks to a full moon and a cloudless sky, we could see almost as well as if it were daytime. Which meant, of course, that we could also be seen. Our shadows were dark and sharp on the pavement. We didn't say much for fear of being heard. Nor did we linger. In fact, we walked so fast, we were almost jogging, ever alert to danger, ever scanning the kudzu for the landmarks on the map.

Oddly, it wasn't the possibility of meeting Silas that frightened me as much as the unknown things that might be hiding in the kudzu—the ones all kids fear. Every monster who'd ever lain in wait under my bed or in my closet had found its way to the Magic Forest—the nightmare forest. Each time the breeze lifted the vines, I expected them to reach out and grab us, plants come to life like the apple trees in *The Wizard of Oz*.

"Shouldn't we have come to the shoe by now?" I whispered.

We walked a little slower, fearing we'd passed it. An owl hooted off to the right somewhere, and the kudzu rustled menacingly, rising up around us like phantoms of the night. I felt goose-bumpy. Anxious. Even Bear was tense.

"There it is." Arthur pointed to what appeared to be the toe of a giant's boot poking out of the kudzu, its yellow paint cracked and peeling. "Now for Mother Hubbard's Cupboard."

"I hope you know where you're going," Danny muttered. "What if he hurts my mother? What if . . ." He looked around at the kudzu raising and lowering its scraggly arms in a breeze. "Man, I hate this place."

We'd come to another fork in the path. Consulting his map, Arthur pointed to the right. "This way."

I looked at the map. "Are you sure?"

"Positive." Arthur hurried ahead of me, his tennis shoes slapping the pavement.

"You'd better be right," Danny said in a sort of threatening way.

I followed Arthur silently, but Bear loped ahead, glancing back now and then to make sure we were still there. The moon glided along beside us, lighting the path but casting everything else into darkness.

After ten or fifteen long minutes, I spotted decaying turrets poking up from the weeds and vines. If I remembered the map right, Cinderella's Castle was in the middle of the park—and nowhere near Mother Hubbard's Cupboard.

I hurried after Arthur. "This isn't right. The castle's straight ahead. We took a wrong turn."

"I knew I shouldn't listen to a loser like you," Danny said.

We ran back the way we'd come. At one point, I tripped on a vine and fell on the very knee I'd scraped in my bike accident. With fresh blood running down my leg, I limped after Arthur, who hadn't even noticed I'd fallen. It occurred to me he was the most self-absorbed person I'd ever known.

"Here's the path," Arthur called. "Hurry up. Are you walking in your sleep or something?"

I didn't waste energy explaining I was injured—no point in giving Danny something to jeer at. Instead, I kept my eyes out for the cupboard. I spotted it before Arthur or Danny, a dilapidated refreshment stand, listing to one side but still sporting a faded sign for frozen custard.

We stopped to study the map again. "Next we look for the Crooked Man's House," Arthur said. "It should be this way."

"Should be?" Danny asked. "*Better* be."

We set off down yet another winding path, overgrown

with weeds and underbrush and kudzu. As usual, Bear trotted ahead, sniffing and turning his head from side to side, as if he were looking, too.

After several minutes, we found what seemed to be the remains of the Crooked Man's House, now a pile of broken beams and shingles. Eagerly, we passed it by, scanning the kudzu for the Dish and the Spoon, our next landmark.

Just around a bend, we spotted the tall wooden Spoon sticking up above the vines, its peeling face ghastly in the moonlight. There was no sign of the Dish, but a headless fiberglass cow lay on the path beside a plastic moon split into two pieces.

"The gingerbread men should be straight ahead," Arthur said.

Deeper in the park than I'd gone before, I stumbled through the weeds behind Arthur and Danny. The darkness seemed darker here, the kudzu taller and thicker. All around us, the breeze made a melancholy sound, and the kudzu leaves lifted and fell.

My heart sped up, and I jumped at every sound—an insect's chirp, a bird's flapping wings, the rustle of small creatures in the undergrowth.

Seemingly unfazed, Arthur hummed and whistled in a tuneless, irritating way and played with the flashlight. He held it under his chin and shone the light upward, making his face into a hideous mask. He swept the beam across bushes and vines and trees.

"Quit shining that thing all over the place," Danny finally said. "You want to tell everybody where we're at?"

Arthur didn't say anything, but he turned the flashlight off and even stopped humming.

Ahead of us, Bear looked back and wagged his tail as if he were encouraging us to follow him. He led us off the path and through a dense thicket of brambles, honeysuckle, and kudzu, tangled into an almost impenetrable barrier.

After stopping a few times to sniff and once to lift his leg, Bear led us to the ruins of the Witch's Hut, almost completely hidden in a jungle of kudzu.

Danny actually grinned. "He's one smart dog, ain't he?"

He started toward the hut, but Arthur grabbed the back of his shirt to stop him. For a second, I thought Danny was going to punch him, but all he said was, "Don't you ever touch me again."

"I just want to make sure nobody's there," Arthur said.

"I was going to do that." Danny said it as if Arthur had tried to stop him from checking out the hut.

The three of us crouched in the kudzu with Bear and surveyed the hut. Despite the broken windows, sagging roof, and rotten boards, the place was still standing. Maybe the tree beside it had protected it from the weather and the worst of the kudzu.

Just as we were about to approach the dark doorway, I grabbed Arthur's arm and pulled him down. My heart was pounding so hard I could hardly speak. "Look," I squeaked, "by the door. A woman."

Arthur tensed for a second and then laughed. "It's the witch—the one I used to think was a real live crazy woman." He stood up, his glasses shining in the moonlight. "I can't believe she's still there."

The witch stood just inside the door, stinking of dampness and decay. Her black dress had rotted into faded tatters, and her green papier-mâché face was crazed with cracks and splotched with mildew. Her hair fell in moth-eaten strings. The arms she'd once waved hung limply by her side. In her current condition, she looked like a corpse propped up to scare visitors away.

"You were scared of that old thing?" Danny laughed. "You really are a wimp."

"I'm not scared of it now," Arthur said. Edging past the witch, he shone his flashlight into the darkness. I glimpsed merry-go-round animals, a fake wishing well, and several teacups the size of small jacuzzis. Stuffing and springs popped out from rips in the teacups' vinyl upholstery.

"Those are the seats from Alice's Tea Party ride," Arthur told me. "The cups spun round and round and up and down—more nauseating than scary." He started to laugh. "I rode it once after lunch and barfed it all—hot dogs, cotton candy, French fries, frozen custard. I must've splattered everyone in a twenty-foot radius. You should've been there, Logan. It was hilarious."

Danny shook his head. "Too bad they didn't have YouTube then. Think of all the hits you would've got. Everybody loves barfing kids."

"We didn't come here to remember the good old days," I said. "Let's find the evidence before Silas shows up."

Paying no attention to me or Danny, Arthur swept his light around the room and stopped on a bunch of larger-than-life wooden figures leaning against a wall—Humpty-Dumpty,

Little Miss Muffet, the Knave of Hearts, Little Bo Peep and her sheep.

"Let's take some of this stuff home," he said. "We could make the coolest haunted house for Halloween—"

I grabbed his arm and pulled him away from Humpty-Dumpty whose mildewed face really did look gruesome enough to scare just about anyone. "Can't you keep your mind on one thing at a time? We're supposed to find the gingerbread men, remember?"

Bear barked outside, and the three of us ran out to see what was going on. The dog had pulled a flat, wooden gingerbread man out of a tangle of vines and weeds. Like the little plastic men, his arms stretched out to either side, and his mouth was open in a big "O." If it hadn't been for the slimy slug trails all over him, he would've been kind of cute.

"There's another one beside him." Arthur struggled to pull kudzu out of the way. Green with moss, the second gingerbread man lay on his back.

With a lot of effort, we uncovered twelve gingerbread men, all fallen flat and rotting under the kudzu.

"Mrs. Donaldson must have buried the briefcase near this one." Arthur stared down at the gingerbread man closest to the hut door—and the witch. "That's why she wrote 'And don't be scared' in the note."

He pulled a bent, rusty trowel out of the pocket of his cargo shorts. While I held the flashlight, he began to dig. Bear stuck his nose in the hole. Soon he was digging, too.

Danny watched the dog with interest. "I bet Grandma took him with her when she buried the briefcase."

"He did seem to know the way," Arthur said.

Suddenly, Bear lifted his head and barked. Arthur shone the flashlight into the hole. A rotten leather handle was sticking out of the dirt.

Pushing Arthur and me aside, Danny lifted the filthy briefcase out carefully and started to fiddle with the rusty catch holding it shut,

Before he got it open, we heard a rustling sound. A snapping branch. A cough. The smell of cigarette smoke. A trace of perfume. Low voices. Someone was coming—at least three people.

Bear lifted his head and bared his teeth. Danny grabbed him. "It must be Silas," he whispered. "And Mom."

"Hide," Arthur whispered. "Don't let them see us."

Clutching the briefcase, Danny followed Arthur and me back into the hut. Hiding behind the stinky old witch, we held Bear tight and waited.

19

O utside, the voices came closer.

"If you've dragged me out here on a wild-goose chase," a man said, "I won't be paying a lawyer to get you out of jail."

"Don't worry," Silas said. "*She* knows where it's at."

"I don't know where it is," Violet said. "And, even if I did, I wouldn't tell *you*."

"This ain't no game," Silas said. "Quit messing with us and show us where it's at."

Danny crept a little closer to the open door and peered around the witch's ragged skirt. "He'd better not hurt her," he whispered. "I'll kill him if he does, I swear I will."

Doing my best to keep Bear quiet, I looked over Danny's shoulder and saw a man, his back to us, facing Silas and Violet.

"Who's that?" I asked.

Danny shook his head. "The last time I saw Silas, he was leaving on his motorcycle. There wasn't nobody with him."

"Give me a minute," Arthur said. "I've heard that voice before."

Outside, Silas raised his voice. "I'm your husband," he said. "You do what I say, when I say it."

"We got a divorce," Violet said. "Or did you forget?"

From the sound of it, Silas gave Violet a hard slap. Danny cussed, and I winced as if Silas had hit me. When Bear growled, Arthur cupped the dog's muzzle in his hands. "Hush," he whispered. "Please, Bear."

"The briefcase belongs to me," the stranger said, "I'd appreciate your giving it to me, Violet."

"Tell the man where it is." Silas hit her again, harder this time.

Beside me Danny doubled his fists and cussed again, using longer and worse words this time. "I'll kill him," he muttered.

Violet looked at the stranger. Her hair hung in her eyes, and a dribble of blood ran from her nose. "I won't tell you anything! Or him, either!"

"Are you going to make me beat the truth out of you?" Silas hit her again. She stumbled backward, and he came after her, fist drawn back, aiming at her face.

With a muffled cry, Danny jumped out from our hiding place and ran toward Silas. "Leave her be!" he shouted, "Don't hurt her!"

Before Silas had time to react, Danny tackled him and knocked him down. At the same moment, Bear broke away from Arthur and me and threw himself on Silas. Losing his grip on Danny, Silas rolled around on the ground, trying to choke the dog. "Get him off me!" he yelled. "Get him off me!"

Without looking at Silas, Violet stumbled toward the hut. "Run," she cried to Arthur and me. "Get the police!"

The third person stepped out of the shadows and into the moonlight. Arthur and I stared at him in disbelief. Mr. DiSilvio—Anthony the perfect one's father. Mr. DiSilvio—sponsor of the soccer team. Mr. DiSilvio—giver of parties. Mr. DiSilvio—embezzler . . . murderer.

"Nobody's going anywhere." Mr. DiSilvio's low voice had a hard edge that scared me more than Silas's shouts and curses. He also had a gun in his hand—which *really* scared me.

"I *told* you there was something fake about that man," Arthur whispered.

Glancing at Danny, Mr. DiSilvio added, "Get that dog under control before I shoot him."

Without a word of protest, Danny grabbed Bear's collar and tried to drag him away from Silas. "Get off!" he shouted. "Get off him. Leave him be!"

Still growling, Bear let go. It was clear he hadn't done all he wanted to do to Silas. Chew his leg off. Kill him. Eat him.

"Look at my jeans!" Silas yelled. "That dog tore the leg half off. He *bit* me. I'm bleeding!"

"Shut up, Silas. I'm tired of your whining." Mr. DiSilvio didn't look at the man as he spoke. Instead, his eyes focused on me. "I told you to stay away from this place, Logan. It's too bad you and your neighbor didn't listen to my advice."

"What are you going to do with us?" Arthur's voice shook, and I was cold all over. I'd never really believed we could be killed in the Magic Forest, but it seemed pretty possible now.

Mr. DiSilvio looked at his gun as if he'd just noticed it was in his hand. "It all depends on Violet," he said softly. "Once she produces my briefcase—the one her mother stole from my office—I'll make a decision."

We looked at her. She folded her arms tightly across her chest as if she were freezing. The blood from her nose had snaked down the front of her T-shirt, leaving a dark streak.

"Stupid female," Silas said. "It's not my fault she won't tell you nothing, Mr. DiSilvio. She's stubborn as a mule and twice as dumb."

"Don't talk about Mom like that," Danny said. "Or I'll—"

"Or you'll what?" Silas punched him so fast no one saw it coming.

Danny reeled backward and lost his grip on Bear's collar. The dog charged at Silas, but this time he was ready. Picking up a fallen branch, Silas swung at Bear. That sent Danny into action again. Getting to his feet, he hurled himself at Silas. Cussing and yelling like a crazy kid, he pummeled his father with his fists. "Leave Bear be! He was Grandma's dog!"

Silas shoved Danny so hard he landed on the ground with a thud that made me wince. "Don't try that again," Silas said, "or I'll bust your head open."

Arthur and I managed to keep Bear from going after Silas, but it took all of our strength.

Mr. DiSilvio looked at us wearily. It was clear he didn't know what to do with any of us. Turning to Violet, he added, "I'm tired of this charade. The briefcase, if you please."

"She don't have it," Danny said. "We dug it up already. It's in there." He pointed at the Witch's Hut. "Take it and let us go."

"Moron!" Arthur clenched his teeth in frustration. "He'll shoot us all now," he muttered to me. "He doesn't have any reason not to."

Mr. DiSilvio strode to the hut. The moment he stepped inside, I heard a shout from the woods.

"I knew you'd be here, Silas!" Billy Jarmon crashed out of the kudzu. "You ain't going nowhere with that money. Not till you give me and Johnny our share."

Johnny was behind Billy. And behind Johnny was Nina. Stunned speechless, I closed my eyes and hoped I'd see someone else when I opened them. But it was still her—Nina Stevens. The look she gave me was anything but friendly. For a second, I thought she was going to march over and shake Arthur and me senseless. Instead, she turned her head away as if she couldn't stand the sight of us. She didn't care what happened to us. Why should she? We were just two kids who'd gotten in her way.

Although it made me sick, I found myself wondering if she'd been in cahoots with Billy and Johnny all along. Maybe she wasn't even a reporter. Maybe she'd played the part so she could ask questions about the murder and the money. For all I knew, she was a Jarmon or a Phelps. After all, she was a liar, a schemer, a crook—just like them.

I wanted to tell her what I thought of her, maybe even cuss her out, but I knew I'd be better off keeping my mouth shut. With any luck, the whole bunch of them would forget about Arthur and me, and we could sneak into the kudzu and run for home.

I watched Johnny saunter into the clearing, but Nina

stayed where she was, as if she were waiting for something to happen.

"Thanks for making so much noise," Johnny told Silas. "We knew you were here somewhere, but if Bear hadn't been barking and you hadn't been yelling and cussing, we never would have found you."

Silas was about to say something when Billy turned on him angrily. "Hey, what happened to Violet? She don't look too good. You been hitting her again?"

"Shut your stupid mouth." Silas gestured at the Witch's Hut. Mr. DiSilvio was standing in the doorway, the briefcase in one hand, the gun in the other.

"I don't want to use this," he said. "So I suggest you all come into the hut and allow me to leave with my briefcase."

"You ain't going nowhere without me," Silas said. "We made a deal."

"The deal didn't include all these people." Mr. DiSilvio waved the gun at Arthur and me, Danny and Violet, Johnny and Billy. So far he hadn't noticed Nina. But she'd noticed him.

"Richard DiSilvio," she said softly, as if she were greeting an old friend.

"Nina." Mr. DiSilvio stared at her, obviously surprised. "What are you doing here?"

"I'm arresting you," she said, holding up a badge that shone like silver in the moonlight. In her other hand was a revolver. "Detective Nina Stevens, Richmond police," she announced. "Drop the gun and the briefcase. Then get on the ground, face-down."

Arthur gasped, and my knees went weak with relief. Nina

wasn't a crook. She wasn't a Jarmon or a Phelps. She was a cop. Nina was a cop. A detective. I could hardly believe it.

If Mr. DiSilvio was surprised, he hid it well. "On what charges?" he asked as if he were inquiring about the score of a baseball game.

Never taking the gun or her eyes off him, Nina said, "Embezzlement, homicide, money laundering, racketeering. Is that enough for now?"

Instead of showing fear or even alarm, Mr. DiSilvio simply sighed. Then, in one quick move, he grabbed Violet and held her in front of him. "I really don't feel like being arrested tonight," he said. "So unless you want an ugly scene, I suggest you—"

"Let her go!" Nina shouted. "You can't get away—the woods are crawling with police."

As she spoke, Danny hurled himself at Mr. DiSilvio. Surprised, the man lost his hold on Violet and the gun. As she fell to the ground, Mr. DiSilvio made a dash for the woods and dove into the kudzu, leaving the vines waving.

"Nobody move!" Nina yelled at the rest of us, but she was too late to stop Silas, Billy, and Johnny. They'd disappeared when Mr. DiSilvio grabbed Violet.

"Stop that man!" Violet cried to Nina. "He killed my mother!"

Nina put an arm around Violet's shoulders. "Don't worry," she said. "He won't get far."

At that moment, an uproar exploded in the woods. Branches snapped, bushes rustled, kudzu swayed, flashlights probed the shadows.

The police, I thought. But I was wrong. At least ten or twelve protesters surged out of the woods, waving SAVE THE MAGIC signs and singing "Follow the Yellow Brick Road," very loudly and incredibly badly. A wheezing accordion accompanied them, along with what sounded like a tuba, a couple of flutes, bagpipes, and several harmonicas.

The Three Bears were right out in front, their arms linked with Goldilocks, Alice in Wonderland, Old King Cole, Mother Goose, Humpty-Dumpty, and Little Bo Peep. Behind them were a fat man in lederhosen playing the accordion and a man in a kilt puffing on a bagpipe.

Barking and growling, Bear doubled and redoubled his efforts to get away from us. Arthur, Danny, and I could barely hold him.

Nina turned on the protesters in amazement, but they were so focused on what they were doing that they didn't even seem to notice her. Or the revolver in her hand. Or her big shiny badge.

A woman wearing a braided yellow wig and a peasant dress ran out of the woods. "There's the Witch's Hut," she cried joyfully. "Just the way I remember it!"

"Are you here for the protest, too?" Humpty-Dumpty asked Violet. She stared at the ground and said nothing.

"Where's your costume?" Little Bo Peep wanted to know.

Violet shook her head and tried to fade into the shadows before anyone noticed her face.

"It doesn't matter what she's wearing," Old King Cole said. "We need help to stop those bulldozers."

Just then a police helicopter roared overhead and shone a

brilliant spotlight on us. An officer with a megaphone shouted, "Nobody move! Stay where you are! This is a crime scene."

"It's the cops," someone yelled. "We're exercising our right to protest! They have no grounds to arrest us!"

Nina stepped up to the protesters. "I'm Detective Nina Stevens," she told them. "The police aren't here for you. Four fugitives are at large in the park. Two of the men are extremely dangerous. I advise you to stay where you are and let us take care of this. If you insist on blundering around in the woods, you'll be charged with interference."

Old King Cole eyed Nina anxiously. "But what about our protest? The bulldozers are scheduled to start in the morning. We have to stop them."

Instead of answering, Nina pulled out a cell phone and began talking to the police in the helicopter.

The protesters milled around, mumbling and muttering and complaining. Some of them wanted to fan out through the park as they'd planned, but most of them just stood there, holding SAVE THE MAGIC signs and looking as glum as grownups dressed in Mother Goose costumes can look.

Danny, Arthur, and I were huddled around Bear doing our best to control him. Violet stood a few feet away, arms still folded tightly across her chest, head down to hide her face, as if she was ashamed that Silas had beaten her.

Danny looked at his mother. "He's not getting away with this," he muttered. With one quick, unexpected move, he yanked Bear away from Arthur and me. Free at last, the dog took off through the crowd of protesters, with Danny close behind him.

A glance at Nina and Violet told us that neither woman had noticed Danny's disappearance. Taking advantage of the restless, noisy crowd of protesters, Arthur and I darted between and around them, hard on Danny's heels.

20

We caught up with Danny near Mother Hubbard's Cupboard. Bear ran to lick our faces, but Danny stared at us angrily. "Why don't you go home and leave me alone?"

"We came to help you catch DiSilvio and Silas," Arthur said.

"I don't need your help. I have Bear—and this." Danny took Mr. DiSilvio's gun out of his pocket. "I'll kill both of them if I have to."

"Where did you get that?" I edged closer to Arthur. There was no telling whom Danny might decide to shoot.

"I picked it up when DiSilvio dropped it," he said.

"You wouldn't kill your own father," Arthur whispered.

"He don't deserve to be anybody's father." Suddenly, Bear raced away, and Danny took off after him. "Wait up, Bear!" he hollered.

Arthur and I chased them, tripping over roots and vines, stumbling down hills, ducking clumps of kudzu. Just ahead, Bear was barking and Danny was yelling. *Please*, I whispered, *please don't let Danny shoot anybody.*

Snuffling with fear, I staggered after Arthur. We broke into a clearing. Mr. DiSilvio stood with his back pressed against a tree, kept there by Bear. Silas was nowhere in sight, and neither was the briefcase. Billy and Johnny weren't there, either.

Danny stood a few feet away, pointing the gun at Mr. DiSilvio. His hands shook, but I was sure he'd pull the trigger if the man moved. "Who killed my grandma?" he shouted. "You or my father?"

Mr. DiSilvio stared at him, making no effort to hide his contempt. "Put that gun down, you little punk."

Danny hurled a few swear words at the man, then repeated his question. "Who killed my grandma?"

Mr. DiSilvio didn't answer. His eyes were cold, but I guessed he was more scared than he let on. He was a ruined man. Nothing could save him now.

Overhead, the police helicopter circled, motor roaring, shining a spotlight down through the treetops. Someone shouted in the woods, and Arthur yelled, "Over here, over here!"

Mr. DiSilvio folded his arms across his chest and sagged against the tree, but Danny held the gun with both hands, the way cops do in movies and on TV. "Answer me, you—" More cussing.

Three policemen in bulletproof vests crashed out of the kudzu. "Put the gun down, son," one shouted.

But Danny kept the gun pointed at Mr. DiSilvio. "Not till he answers me!"

"Are you crazy?" Arthur yelled. "Do what he says. He'll shoot you if you don't."

The cop scowled at Arthur. I guessed he didn't think of

himself as the kind of man who shot twelve-year-old kids, even if they did have guns and were named Phelps.

At that moment, Violet ran out of the woods, screaming at the cops. "Don't shoot him, he's just a child."

By now, Danny was crying. Snot dripped from his nose. His hands shook so badly, he couldn't keep the gun pointed at Mr. DiSilvio. "He deserves to die," he wailed.

The cop walked over to Danny and took the gun from him. "We'll take care of him, son."

Violet tried to hug Danny, but he pulled away from her. "I'm not a child," he yelled through his tears.

Meanwhile, Bear stood guard, snarling, the fur on his back standing up. He was so fixated on Mr. DiSilvio, he hadn't even noticed the police.

"Whose dog is that?" a cop asked.

I noticed he was holding a stun gun. Scared for Bear's safety, Arthur, Danny, and I ran to the dog. Somehow we managed to haul him back on his hind legs, still straining to get at Mr. DiSilvio. It took all three of us to hold him.

With Bear out of the way, the cops moved in, cuffed Mr. DiSilvio, read him his rights, and led him away. As they shoved him out of the clearing, he glanced over his shoulder at Arthur, Danny, and me. He didn't need to say anything. The anger in his eyes spoke for itself. For our own good, I hoped he was facing life with no parole.

"Did you get Silas?" Arthur asked the remaining cop.

Before the cop could answer, Bear broke away from us and tore into the underbrush. All three of us ran after the dog. If anyone could find Silas, it was Bear.

"Come back here!" the cop yelled after us.

"Danny!" Violet wailed.

But we'd already zigged and zagged and vanished into the kudzu. It sounded as though the cop tried to follow us, but judging by the noise he made, he fell down. We heard him thrashing around in the kudzu and shouting. Overhead, the helicopter circled so low, the kudzu danced a spooky jig in the wind from the blades. The noise made it hard to hear anything else.

With us on his heels, Bear headed down the path that led to Willie the Whale. We thudded across the rainbow bridge straight into a crowd of protesters gathered around the whale's dark pond.

"Get the cops!" Old King Cole hollered at us. "He's inside the whale!"

Bear tried to charge through the excited protesters, but they didn't make way fast enough. Arthur and I managed to grab his collar and stop him.

"You'd better come out!" Alice in Wonderland cried into Willie's gaping mouth. I noticed she was clutching a stuffed white rabbit.

The Knave of Hearts seized Alice's hand and pulled her away from the whale. "What if he's got a gun?" he shouted. "The detective said he was dangerous. Didn't you hear her?"

Danny pushed his way through the crowd and stopped in front of the whale. "Come outta there!" he yelled. "They got you now—you ain't going nowhere but jail."

If Silas answered, he was drowned out by at least a dozen

cops charging out of the woods. "Clear the area!" they shouted. "Clear the area!"

Behind them came Nina and Violet. While the protesters moved slowly back from Willie, Nina pulled Danny away and handed him over to Violet. "Keep him under control," she said, as if Danny was a raging pit bull or something.

With guns drawn, the cops approached the whale. "Come out with your hands up, Phelps!" one yelled. "We've got you surrounded."

There was a scuffling sound inside Willie. His fiberglass sides shook a little. Slowly the vines covering the whale's mouth moved aside, and Silas crawled out. His eyes sought Danny.

"Tell 'em, son. I was just down here to join up with them protesters," he said. "Ain't no need to arrest me. I got that freedom-of-speech thing—just like everybody else." As proof, he held up a SAVE THE MAGIC sign he'd found somewhere.

At that moment, a news photographer stepped out of the crowd and began taking pictures. I noticed Arthur moving a little closer to the action. He was still determined to be in the paper.

"I'm not lying for you, not after what you did to Mom!" Danny yelled at his father. "And either you or that rich dude killed my grandma. I hope both of you get the chair."

Silas gave Danny a look of such pure ugliness, I wondered how he stood it. If my dad ever looked at me like that, I would have melted like ice cream on a hot sidewalk.

"Shush," Violet whispered, still holding Danny tight. "Let the police handle this."

We watched an officer read Silas his rights, cuff him, and lead him away.

I turned to high-five Arthur, but he wasn't beside me. In fact, I didn't see him anywhere. Not talking to the cops, not talking to reporters, not posing for pictures. Just as I was getting worried, he crawled out of Willie's mouth with a big grin on his face. In his hand was the briefcase.

"Silas hid it under a pile of leaves," he told us. "He must have planned on coming back for it."

"Ha," I said. "He's not coming back here or any other place for a long, long time. Hopefully never."

"Let's give the briefcase to Violet," Arthur said. "She should have it."

Violet was sitting on a dilapidated bench beside Danny. Bear lay at their feet, but he looked up and thumped his tail when he saw us coming.

The first gray light of dawn lit Violet's face, showing the bruises Silas had given her. One eye was swollen shut. Her upper arms were black and blue, and her T-shirt was torn at the shoulder and stained with blood from her nose. She'd never had a happy face, but now she looked sadder than ever.

Arthur laid the briefcase in Violet's lap as if it were a holy offering. She stared at in disbelief. "You found it," she whispered. A real smile lit her face, and she flung her arms around him. "Thank you, Arthur, thank you!"

Arthur blushed, and Danny groaned in embarrassment, but I was just plain happy to see that smile on Violet's face.

Violet fumbled with the briefcase's rusty old catch and lifted the lid. On top was a pink envelope and an ordinary five-subject spiral notebook, the sort you'd use in school. Under that were bundles of bills, more money than I'd ever seen in my life. Thousands—millions, maybe. It was unbelievable.

Too stunned to speak, we sat there and stared at the money. No one touched it, not even Danny.

With care, Violet plucked the envelope out of the briefcase. Inside were two things: a note from Mrs. Donaldson and a green plastic gingerbread man. Holding the little man in one hand, Violet read her mother's words out loud.

"Dearest Violet,

This is Richard DiSilvio's briefcase. It contains over two million dollars, which he embezzled over a period of years from the Magic Forest and other businesses in Bealesville. The notebook contains the records he kept of his criminal activities.

"I think Silas is somehow involved, but I'm not sure how. Maybe he does Mr. DiSilvio's dirty work. Someone must.

"If anything happens to me, one of them is responsible. Take the briefcase to the police. I know Mr. DiSilvio's an important man, and he's done a lot for Bealesville, but the fact is he's a criminal. And a dangerous man. Be careful, Violet. Keep yourself and the children safe.

"I love you."

Mrs. Donaldson had signed her name with a flourish. Beneath it, she'd added:

"P.S. Here is the twelfth gingerbread man, which you have earned by retrieving the briefcase."

As Violet finished reading her mother's note, she began to cry. Danny patted her shoulder and mumbled things I couldn't quite hear. They might have been descriptions of awful things he wanted to do to Silas and Mr. DiSilvio. Or they might have been attempts to comfort his mother. Knowing Danny, who could tell?

Nina left a group of police and sat down beside Violet. "Is that what I think it is?" she asked in a soft voice.

Violet showed her the briefcase, the notebook, and the money. "It's the proof you need. And look—Mr. DiSilvio's initials are on the lid. See?" She pointed to three faded gilt letters, R. J. D.

Nina reached for the briefcase. "What's in your hand?" she asked Violet.

"Just a note from my mother," Violet said. "And this." She held out her hand, palm-up, and showed Nina the little gingerbread man.

"I'll need those, too," Nina said gently.

Violet closed her fist around the gingerbread man and pressed the note to her chest. "You can't take these. There're from my mother—"

"I'm sorry," Nina said. "It's evidence."

"Please."

"If possible, I'll have the little plastic figure returned to you. I imagine the police will keep the letter. If you wish, I'll make a copy for you."

Violet nodded silently and let Nina take everything. "There was another letter," she said, "but Silas took it."

Arthur reached deep into his pockets and took out a wadded-up sheet of paper. "Here's the copy Logan and I made."

"Thank you, Arthur." Nina smiled at him in the old way, charming me all over again.

"So who killed my grandmother?" Danny broke in, "Mr. DiSilvio or my—my—" It seemed the word "father" had gotten stuck in his throat, and he just couldn't say it.

Nina patted his shoulder. "We can't be sure until both men are tried." Turning to Arthur and me, she said, "I've talked to your parents, Logan, and your grandmother, Arthur. It's time to take you both home."

A policeman stepped forward and offered Violet and Danny a ride to Wal-Mart so she could get her car. Bear followed them into the back seat.

"Hey," Arthur yelled at the dog. "Come back here."

Danny looked out the window at us, his scowl firmly in place. "Told ya—he's my dog," he snarled. "I'm taking him home. To my house. Just try and stop me."

"He won't stay," Arthur said. "Bear's used to a higher standard of living."

"You'll see." Danny rolled up the window, and the police car drove away.

"*You'll* see," Arthur muttered.

Nina put a hand on our shoulders. "You know you've been incredibly foolish."

Arthur's chin jutted out. "We had to get that briefcase before the bulldozers came."

"It would have been safer and much more sensible to go to the police," Nina said.

"If we'd known you were a detective," I said, "maybe—"

"And maybe not." Arthur was angry, I could tell.

"What do you mean?" Nina asked.

"You told Logan's mother a lot of stuff about me," he said. "Mrs. Forbes used to like me a lot, even invited me to eat dinner at their house, but now she hates me—just because of what *you* told her."

To keep from looking at Arthur, I started scratching an itchy place on my leg. He had no idea how Mom actually felt about him. Which was just as well.

"Listen to me, Arthur." Nina lifted his chin and forced him to look at her. "Your boy-detective routine was getting in the way of a criminal investigation. I thought if I broke you two up, you'd stay out of the Magic Forest and I'd be free to get on with my work without having to worry about you."

"You didn't have to tell Mrs. Forbes lies."

Nina sighed. "I'll talk to Logan's mom," she told Arthur. "I'll say I was 'misinformed.'"

He shrugged and shoved his hands into his pockets. From the look on his face, I guessed he didn't have much faith in Nina.

To change the subject, I tugged Nina's arm. "What happened to Billy and Johnny? Did they get caught, too?"

Nina shook her head. "They managed to slip away in the confusion. But don't worry, we'll find them."

On the way out of the park, a gang of reporters came running over. "Are these the boys who found the evidence?" one asked while another thrust a camera in our faces.

It seemed they'd already talked to Violet and Danny, but they wanted to hear the story from us. Arthur did most of the talking. Using his fanciest vocabulary words, he exaggerated everything, especially the part where we'd faced down Mr. DiSilvio. Even though Nina tried to correct his most outlandish claims, the reporters were pretty impressed with Arthur's heroic actions.

After about half an hour, Nina managed to pry us away.

"At least they were *real* reporters." Arthur gave Nina a sidewise look. "And we really will be in the newspaper this time."

Nina didn't even blush.

21

In the parking lot, I expected to see the bulldozers revved up and ready to go, but they sat there silently, not a hard hat in sight.

"What will happen to the Magic Forest now?" Arthur asked.

"The owner of the property is in jail," Nina said. "Nothing can be done with the land until the case against Mr. DiSilvio is resolved."

Arthur grinned and high-fived me. "The Magic Forest is saved—at least for now!"

Nina settled Arthur in the front seat and me in the back, started the engine, and turned on the air conditioner. At first, all it did was blow hot air, but by the time we were heading up the first hill on Route 23, a nice stream of cool air blew on me.

"Our bikes!" Arthur suddenly squawked. "We left them in the woods."

With amazing patience, Nina drove back and waited while Arthur and I retrieved our bikes. She opened the trunk, and we laid them carefully inside, trying not to do anything ungrateful like scratching her car.

The ride home was pretty quiet. For one thing, I was totally exhausted. I'd never been up all night in my life. Nor had I ever seen a loaded gun or run so much or been so scared. All I wanted was to go to bed and sleep until Mom and Dad got over being mad.

Even Arthur didn't have much to say, except for a few questions about Nina's global navigation system. "Grandma would love to have one of those," he said. "She gets lost all the time. Soon she'll need a map to find the back door."

As we turned the corner onto my street, I saw a welcoming party waiting on the porch—Mom, Dad, and Mrs. Jenkins. No one was smiling. They just sat there in a grim row, like a jury about to announce a guilty verdict.

The scene was about as bad as I'd thought it would be. Maybe even worse. Our bikes were confiscated. We were scolded until we felt like worms drying up on a sidewalk after a rainstorm. We were sent to our rooms to bake in the heat.

But true to her word, Nina somehow managed to convince Mom that she'd been wrong about Arthur. I can't say Mom totally changed her opinion of Arthur, but she managed to tolerate him.

By the next day, she'd definitely changed her opinion of the DiSilvio family. "I never trusted that woman," she claimed. "The pretentious house, the luxury cars, the designer clothes, the lady bountiful act. I suspected something not quite legal was going on." She smiled at me. "I'm glad you had the sense to stay away from Anthony."

Dad said nothing, but he winked at me—another moment of male bonding.

• • •

Arthur and I gave our statements to the police, our pictures appeared in the paper, and we even got on *Live-Action Evening News,* along with Danny, who was as unfriendly as ever. He also made a big deal about *his* dog, the biggest hero of all.

The cops arrested Johnny and Billy in Richmond. They, too, showed up on *Live-Action Evening News,* walking from the police car to the courthouse. Johnny hid his face with his hands, but Billy stared into the camera with a scowl mean enough to scare small children.

Dad sighed. "Too bad Johnny got mixed up in this. I was counting on him to help me with those house repairs."

"I don't think he and Billy did anything *too* bad," I said. "They just have a bad reputation, you know? So maybe . . ." My thoughts trailed off. What did I know about the law?

Later in the week, *The Bealesville Post* ran a story about Silas. He claimed Mrs. Donaldson had died by accident. He didn't push her down the steps. She fell trying to get away from him. The reporter quoted him as saying, "She was my mother-in-law. Why would I want to kill her? All she had to do was give me the briefcase."

In the same article, we read that Mr. DiSilvio had hired a big-time lawyer who was advising him to plea-bargain. So far, he hadn't admitted anything.

With the bad guys in jail, the only thing that really worried Arthur and me was Bear. After days had passed with no sign of him, we decided Danny must have him chained up some-where. Otherwise, he'd have come back.

One hot afternoon, a day or so before school started, we rode our bikes to the Phelps place. Violet's car was gone, and the mobile home's shades were down. If it hadn't been for the loud rock music, I'd have thought no one was there.

"Violet must be at work," Arthur said. "And Bear's probably locked up inside."

Dumping his bike in the weeds, he walked across the sun-baked, dusty yard. As usual, I—the spineless wonder—followed him.

At the door, Arthur pressed his face against the rusty screen and shouted, "Bear!"

The dog rushed toward us and butted the screen door open. He was all over Arthur and me, wagging his tail, jumping, licking our faces. I swear he almost knocked us off the mobile home's little porch.

"Get away from him!" Danny came running from somewhere inside and grabbed Bear's collar. "I told you, he's *my* dog now."

"Says who?" Arthur stuck out his skinny little chest and looked Danny in the eye, just asking to get himself killed.

"Says *me*." Danny scowled at us. "He belonged to my grandma, and now he's mine. Mom said I could keep him."

"But *my* grandma's been taking care of him ever since your grandma died," Arthur said.

Bear looked from Danny to Arthur and back again, grinning and wagging his tail.

"Get outta here." Danny yanked Bear inside the mobile home. He was about to slam the door in our faces. But Arthur stuck his foot out and stopped him.

"Let Bear choose who he wants to live with," he suggested. "Turn him loose. If he comes with us, he's ours. If he stays here, he's yours."

I didn't think Danny would go along with that idea, but he surprised me. "Good boy," he whispered to Bear, "good boy. You stay here with me, okay?" Then he let the dog go.

Bear ran to Arthur and me and wagged his tail. With the dog behind us, we dashed across the yard, shouting encouragement to him.

Behind us, Danny yelled, "Bear, Bear, come back!"

It was the saddest call I'd ever heard. In fact, if I hadn't wanted the dog so badly, I would've felt sorry for Danny Phelps.

Yanking our bikes out of the weeds, we hopped on and started pedaling downhill. Lance Armstrong couldn't have caught us.

At the bottom of the hill, we waited for Bear to catch up with us. He was standing on the top of the hill, wagging his tail, but when we called him, he turned around and headed back to Danny.

"Great idea," I told Arthur.

He looked at me sadly. "I thought he'd come with us, I really did."

"Me, too."

We rode home without talking, each of us thinking about Bear. I hoped he'd change his mind someday and choose us. But I had a feeling I'd better not count on it.

Two days later, school started. The big yellow bus was already crowded when we got on.

"What was it like to have a gun pointed at you?" an eighth-grade boy asked. "Were you scared? Did you think he'd kill you?"

Before we could answer, his friend said, "I think the scariest part of all is being in the Magic Forest with Danny Phelps. That kid is a major wacko."

Everybody laughed, but Arthur said, "Danny was the one who caught DiSilvio."

"He couldn't have done it without Bear," I put in.

But the kids went right on asking questions as if they hadn't even heard what we'd said about Bear and Danny. Somebody wanted to know why Silas had been holding a SAVE THE MAGIC sign. Before we could answer him, a girl asked if I'd ever seen Mrs. Donaldson's ghost. Her friend said she didn't believe in ghosts but had seen one once. Which didn't make any sense to me.

On and on they went. A really cute girl said we were brave. A boy said he wished he'd been with us. His friend said someone should make a movie of it. And, he added, he could star in it because they'd want someone better-looking than Arthur and me.

"My mom's a teller at the bank," a girl said, "and she told me the DiSilvios are bankrupt. They owed money like you wouldn't believe." She chomped her gum. "Mrs. DiSilvio put their house up for sale, and she and Anthony moved to Richmond."

Everybody pretended to moan and groan about how much they'd miss Anthony the perfect one.

"My father says Mr. DiSilvio's nothing but a racketeer," a

girl with a long brown ponytail said. She paused and looked around the bus. "Dad's a cop. So he should know, shouldn't he?"

"I always thought Anthony was a phony," her friend said. "Acting like he was better than everybody else, him and his friends."

The policeman's daughter said, "I bet Anthony's not the only kid in Fair Oaks with a crooked dad."

By the time we got to school, Arthur and I felt like heroes. Until we got off the bus, that is, and saw Danny walking toward us, looking as mean as ever.

"How's Bear?" Arthur asked.

"Fine." Danny looked at us. "He's my dog. You're not getting him back."

"Yeah, I know," Arthur said. "My grandmother said I can pick out a dog at the pound."

"My mom is close—really close—to saying I can get one, too," I put in.

"There won't ever be a dog as good as Bear," Danny said.

A little silence fell. Danny was right. It was too bad we didn't know how to clone Bear.

"Funny about Anthony and me," Danny said suddenly.

"Funny?" I was puzzled. "Funny how?"

"Not ha-ha funny," he said. "Weird funny. Crazy funny. Me and him both having dads in jail. Who'd have thought such a thing?"

"Maybe you two will end up best buddies when you visit your dads in prison," Arthur said.

"I don't know about that jerk Anthony," Danny said, "but I ain't going near a prison."

"How come?" Arthur asked. "Are you scared they'll keep you there?"

Danny's squinty eyes turned dangerous. "Watch your mouth, or you'll get your teeth knocked out."

Showing some sense for once, Arthur stepped back. "Sorry," he mumbled.

Danny shoved his hands in his pockets. I noticed he was wearing new jeans and a clean T-shirt. He'd also gotten a haircut. In fact, he looked a lot better than usual.

"Tell you what, Arthur," he said. "You did good that night at the Magic Forest. Don't tell anybody I cried, and I won't beat up on you no more."

Without giving Arthur a chance to answer, Danny walked over to join his friends. One of them looked at us and laughed, but Danny shook his head.

"As if I'd ever tell on him," Arthur said.

"Who'd believe you if you did?" I asked.

The bell rang then, and Arthur and I joined the crowd of kids lined up to go inside. Ahead of us, one of the girls on the bus was telling her friend that she'd sat near me on the bus— the cute boy who was in the newspaper.

I smiled. So far, things at school were off to a pretty good start. I sure hoped they'd stay that way.

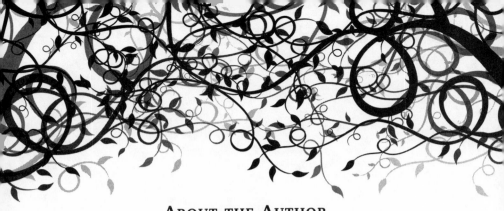

ABOUT THE AUTHOR
MARY DOWNING HAHN

A former children's librarian, Ms. Hahn is among the most versatile and popular novelists for young people today. They respond to her masterly storytelling, and have honored her with more than 48 child-voted state awards. Her recent novels for Clarion Books include *The Old Willis Place* and *Deep and Dark and Dangerous*. Ms. Hahn makes her home in Columbia, Maryland.